To April,
Best Wishes

Part of Me

DEANNA KAHLER

Deanna Kahler
♡

Cover by SelfPubBookCovers.com/Saphira
Author photo by Steven Jon Horner Photography

ISBN: 1545529256
ISBN-13: 978-1545529256

DEDICATION

To my two favorite girls:
my amazing daughter Katie and awesome niece Ashley.
May you follow your own path
and always be true to yourself.

CONTENTS

ACKNOWLEDGMENTS

Everyone who has inspired me to write has shaped me into the person I am today. I am deeply grateful to you all! Thank you for your endless encouragement, praise, mentoring, criticism, and most of all, your belief in me. Without you, I would have never attempted the huge (and often insane) job of being an author.

A special thanks to my incredible daughter, Katie, who never ceases to amaze me, and my husband Paul for sticking by me through all life's ups and downs. My sincere gratitude goes to Claire Ashgrove and her awesome editing team for helping to bring the best version of this story forward. And finally, thank you to my fans and followers for reading and giving me a reason to continue writing books.

CHAPTER 1
PLANE SIGHT

Is this how my life ends?

Chase clutched the armrest as the plane shook violently. His heart pounded, and he began to sweat. Outside the window, bright flashes of lightning and endless darkness took over the sky. A sudden and unexpected loud crash of thunder jolted him straighter in his seat.

"Ladies and Gentleman," the pilot called out from the loud speaker. "Please fasten your safety belts and remain in your seats. We are experiencing some turbulence due to the approaching storm."

Chase looked over at his girlfriend Kaitlyn, who sat next to him. She slept as peacefully as an angel despite the bumpy ride. Soft ringlets of blonde hair rested delicately on her shoulders, and he could almost hear the sound of her breath escaping as her chest slowly moved in and out. Across the aisle, Chase's best friends, Kyle and Joe, munched on peanuts and drank Pepsi while they played a game of poker on a tray table. His other friend, Ashley, sat next to them with her nose buried in a book. The corners of her mouth were turned up slightly in pleasure, which made Chase think she was enjoying a romance novel. No one seemed bothered by the rocky journey.

No one except him.

He took a deep breath and tried to think of happy memories to distract himself. It had been a good school year—well, on the surface anyway. He and the guys had played football for the last time as high schoolers. Chase had scored four touchdowns this season and helped the team snag second place overall for its division. Afterward, they celebrated at Dairy Queen with banana splits and parfaits, followed by a party at Joe's house. Chase didn't stay long. Parties had never been his thing. He preferred quiet times such as the many days he spent at Lincoln and Dodge parks, wandering the trails and skipping rocks across the gentle ponds and streams.

And then there was Kaitlyn. They'd been best friends for years but recently took their relationship to the next level. All the guys at school wanted to date her and said Chase was the luckiest guy around. But trapped deep inside his soul was a fear and an aching no one could seem to penetrate, not even his devoted girlfriend.

He was conflicted, torn between who everyone else thought he should be and who he was desperately trying to become. Often, he didn't even recognize himself, which left him feeling confused, lonely, and different.

His life wasn't right, and he had to do something about it—fast. In a little over a month, he'd be graduating from high school, so it was crucial he figured out his place in life. He needed to find himself and determine what made him happy. But how?

Chase drummed his fingers on his leg. His face burned and his palms were clammy. The plane continued to shake as his stomach did a wave of flip-flops. A torrential downpour now slammed against the aircraft. Its sound reminded him of thousands of bullets hitting cold, hard metal. When he heard the drops smash against the plane, chills of dread rippled through his body, a sensation he was all too familiar with.

Here we go again. Much like it did every time he was in or near an airplane, his mind traveled to a frightening place he had never seen, but knew so well.

The pilot announced they were experiencing mechanical difficulties and would be forced to land at the nearest airport. Chase gazed out the window, like he had done a few minutes ago as the storm brewed. Outside, a breathtaking view captivated him. To be so high above the earth, to soar to places men once only dreamed of, was an exhilarating feeling. But the hint of alarm in the pilot's voice reminded him of the brutal truth: his life was not really in his hands; it was an illusion he'd created to help him feel safe.

Within a few minutes, smoke curled outside the window. Just a little at first, and then it slowly built up like a dense fog rolling in, threatening to block out all he knew and loved.

He watched helplessly as the gray, billowing clouds danced across the wings. They called to him, and he could do nothing to resist. "Chase, we've come for you. It's time. Join us now."

Orange flames spiked from the engine. Chase's whole world spun into a dizzying frenzy of fear. The plane dropped sharply, and then plummeted toward the earth below. For a moment, time stood still as he awaited his unfortunate fate. Like a movie playing in slow motion, he became numb. The descent ended when the plane hit the ground in an explosion of fiery fragments. Then everything went black.

Chase shook uncontrollably in his seat and let out a moan.

"Dude, are you okay?" Kyle called from across the aisle.

Chase swallowed hard and struggled to respond. "Yeah," he croaked.

Deep inside, he knew he was not okay. He had never been okay. The nightmares and visions had come on with a vengeance at the age of six. Now, at seventeen, they were as much a part of his life as school, girls, and football—maybe even more so.

Sometimes the images would appear when he saw a plane fly overhead; other times he would be overcome with fear as he watched a news story about a crash. Everywhere he went, something or someone brought on the panic, a familiar yet dreadful, heart-pounding, cold-sweating, body-shaking sensation. Nighttime was the worst. Alone in the dark shadows of his bedroom, he became a helpless victim. The moment he closed his eyes, the fear settled in, threatening to tear him apart like a shark with fierce jaws.

He had tried therapy, without success. The psychologist had said he suffered from Post Traumatic Stress Disorder triggered by his dad's death in a plane crash when he was young. Since then, panic attacks, disturbing images, and violent nightmares had plagued him.

Only the psychologist was wrong about the cause of his distress. There was something else; something he'd missed. Chase had never told him how wrong he was.

His body continued to tremble; his pulse thumped strongly in his neck. He struggled to breathe. *Why must I suffer this way?* He stared at the droplets sliding down his window until they became blurry streaks.

In the midst of his distress, an image of a beautiful woman with flowing brown hair appeared in his head. Her brown eyes fixed on him with a look of sheer terror as if she were reflecting back his own distraught state of mind. He'd seen her before, many times, in his head and in his dreams, although he'd never met anyone who matched her appearance. He wanted to reach out and hug her. He longed to comfort her and tell her everything would be okay, and even more, he wanted her to tell him he would be okay, too.

Chase wiped his sweaty palms on his jeans and let out a deep sigh.

Kaitlyn, now awake, put her hand on his knee and gave it a squeeze. "It's happening again, isn't it?"

Her forehead wrinkled, and her blue eyes looked

teary. Chase wondered if she thought he was crazy.

"Yes," he whispered.

She stroked his hand. "You really should try to get to the bottom of this. I mean, this isn't good for you. It isn't good for us. We're supposed to be having fun and enjoying our spring break. This is one of the most exciting times in our lives. We're seniors, for God's sake. Don't you even care?"

Blood rushed to Chase's cheeks. He clenched the bottom of his seat and pulled himself up straighter. Kaitlyn had snapped him back to reality. She always had a way of disrupting the cycle. If only she knew what he was really going through. To Kaitlyn, a crisis was having a bad hair day or not being popular enough. Sometimes, Chase wasn't even sure she understood real pain.

"Come off it now," he snapped. "Everything isn't all about you. And life isn't one big party."

"All I'm saying—"

"I know what you're saying. My problems get in the way of *your* fun. They aren't convenient for you."

She threw her hands in the air and shot him a look.

"Get over yourself, Kaitlyn. You have no idea how much I suffer. It's horrible. Some days I want to die."

"Well, you don't have to be a jerk about it!"

Chase bowed his head and stared down at his hands until his eyes became blurry. Kaitlyn was right. He was being rather harsh. They had both been on edge lately. Their new relationship status, their big trip, their upcoming graduation, his panic attacks. It was all a bit overwhelming.

He regained his composure and turned to Kaitlyn. "I'm sorry," he said softly. "I didn't mean to upset you. I wish you could understand."

Her expression changed, and she calmly took his hand in hers. The press of her fingers was warm and comforting.

"Look," she said, peering deep into his eyes. "I'm worried about you. Tell me what you need. I'll help in any way I can. I mean it."

"Thanks." He squeezed her hand.

Despite her superficial exterior, Kaitlyn did actually have a heart. Every once and a while, Chase saw her true essence, the part she kept hidden for fear of not being liked or accepted. Kaitlyn embodied much more than what others saw, and her compassionate spirit drew him to her. His decision to start dating her had seemed like an easy one at the time. She was a great girl, and he enjoyed hanging with her. They were best friends. And she was beautiful. What more could he ask for? Their union should have been perfect. But he couldn't shake the feeling something was missing in his life.

"I appreciate your support, Kate." He stroked her hand. "I really do want to enjoy our trip."

"Then why don't you? Why get caught up in something that isn't even real?" She brushed a strand of her highlighted blonde hair away from her face.

Real? It certainly felt real. Although Chase did not believe the nightmares and images he saw were his own experiences, knowing didn't take away their power. What he saw and what he felt profoundly affected him, often sending him into a downward spiral overflowing with intense fear and anguish. In those moments, he was truly lost.

"It's not so simple."

Kaitlyn sighed. "Having fun isn't simple? What's so hard about it?"

"My life is…complicated."

"Is that why you seem so distant with me lately? You still haven't even told me you love me. Do you?"

There it was. The dreaded question. They'd gone out for about six months, and he'd always avoided the topic of love. He enjoyed Kaitlyn's company. They got along great and had a strong, solid friendship. But love?

The plane shook again, and Chase flung his head against the seat back. Beads of sweat ran down his forehead. Kaitlyn didn't seem to notice. She was wrapped up in herself once again.

"You know," she continued. "I can have any guy I want."

Here comes the guilt trip. "Believe me, I know." Chase wiped his forehead and took some deep breaths.

"But I chose *you.* If you don't appreciate me, then I can find someone who does."

He thought carefully before responding. Girls always said they wanted the truth, but they didn't really. They only wanted to hear it if it was good news. He couldn't tell her he loved her. To say so would be a lie. But he couldn't tell her he didn't, either, because he wasn't sure. Truthfully, the closest he had come to experiencing something that felt like love was when he dreamed of the mysterious brown-haired woman. Should he tell Kaitlyn about his dreams? No. She would likely be hurt and confused. How could she understand something he didn't fully comprehend himself?

"Maybe you don't appreciate *me*," he answered finally.

A tear formed in the corner of her eye. "You still didn't answer my question."

Chase looked down at his Nike tennis shoes and said nothing. He studied the white laces and followed the zigzag pattern between the top and bottom of the shoe in a desperate attempt to distract himself. He really had no idea what to say and was irritated at her for putting him on the spot—especially now, when he was already in the middle of distress and turmoil.

Slowly, he looked up and peered out the window into the blackness. The storm seemed to have calmed down a bit, but he was anything but calm. His heart raced as he struggled to find the right words. Kaitlyn deserved more than the silent treatment.

"How am I supposed to know?" he answered finally. "We're only seventeen."

"Well, I love you," she said, tossing back her hair and sticking out her chest.

The plane shook slightly, and Chase's body trembled again. He wasn't sure if it was from the turbulence or what she'd said. Either way, he was afraid. Life for him seemed more challenging than it was for most teenagers. Sure, they all had struggles but he was different. Visions of a natural disaster he'd never witnessed tormented him, and he suffered frequently from intense and debilitating panic attacks. And now, on what was supposed to be a fun and relaxing trip, he fought to maintain some sense of normalcy while Kaitlyn pressured him to admit to feelings he didn't know if he had. It was all too much.

His face became hot once again and his hands tingled. His chest tightened, making breathing a chore. He wanted to jump from his seat and exit the plane, which was impossible considering they were in midair. *Keep it together. You can do this.*

He became lightheaded and woozy, a sure sign he had been hyperventilating. He grabbed the paper trash bag that hung from the back of the seat in front of him and cupped it around his mouth and nose. He breathed slowly and deeply as he watched the bag inflate and deflate. He continued to focus on his slow breathing and tried to block out everything going on around him.

The gentle rhythm of the bag moving in and out soothed him, and his unhurried breaths brought him a sense of calmness. After a few minutes, he was ready to speak again.

"Are you even listening to me?" asked Kaitlyn, who had apparently been talking the whole time. "I told you I loved you."

"You love everybody," he pointed out. "What about Brandon? Wasn't he the love of your life before we started dating? And don't forget about Justin. You were head over heels for him. You even told everyone the two of you were going to get married after high school."

She gasped. "You're not being fair."

"Hey, you two lovebirds," Joe called. "What's going on over there? What's with the unhappy faces? This is spring break. It's time to paaarttyyy!"

"Chase doesn't love me," Kaitlyn said, pouting.

"I never said—" Chase objected.

"You didn't have to," she interrupted. "It's written all over your face."

"Oh, come on now," Joe said. "Let's not get all caught up in this mushy stuff. We're here for one reason and one reason only: to have a good time."

"Joe's right," Kyle piped in. "We're on a plane headed to Panama City. No school. No parents. Total freedom. It's all about us."

Chase suddenly felt a bit guilty for the way he had been talking to Kaitlyn. This was their big trip before high school graduation. A time they'd dreamed of throughout their high school years. He certainly didn't want to ruin Kaitlyn's fun. Besides, spring break was a perfect opportunity to spend some time with his best friends before they ventured into adulthood. After graduation, they would go off to college and possibly drift apart. Who knew where their paths would take them once they were on their own in the world? They had to seize the moment and enjoy their friendship now.

"Kate, you know you're my best friend," he said. "And I do care about you."

He kissed her softly on the cheek, which brought a small, hopeful smile to her face.

"Maybe you love me and don't even know it yet," she said.

Chase shrugged. He didn't want to start any arguments or debate his feelings for her. Everyone thought he belonged with Kaitlyn, including her. They seemed so certain of it. He, on the other hand, really wasn't sure where he belonged and hoped to find out someday. Why was he so lost and confused?

The plane slowed down a bit, much like he had after breathing in the bag.

"Ladies and Gentleman," the pilot announced. "We are beginning our descent and will land at the Northwest Florida Beaches International Airport shortly. Please remain in your seats and be sure your seatbelts are buckled. The storms have passed and the weather forecast for Panama City today is sunny and eighty-two degrees. It's going to be a beautiful day."

"Beautiful like you," Chase whispered in Kaitlyn's ear.

She flashed him a dazzling grin.

"Panama City, here we come!" exclaimed Kyle.

Joe and Kyle gave each other high fives.

"Oooh baby…it's parrrtty time!" Joe cried out.

"I'm happy to be spending spring break with you," Kaitlyn said to Chase.

She leaned over and kissed his lips, and his pulse quickened. As they touched, an image of the mysterious dream woman appeared in his head. She smiled at him and gazed with longing eyes he could easily get lost in. She reached out and stroked his face. Then she pulled him close and kissed him like they were meant for each other.

Who was this woman and why did he keep seeing her?

CHAPTER 2
LONG LOST LOVE

Willow carefully unpacked the last box as she settled into her new apartment. Years of searching had led her here, to a place only a couple of miles from where he lived. She had missed him tremendously, and the ache in her heart had never gone away since they were cruelly separated. He was her one and only love, and she would never be whole again until they were reunited.

She pulled out a few precious mementos: a worn and weathered pink stuffed bunny and tiny pair of baby shoes; her grandfather's gold watch. Next, she retrieved a pewter-framed picture of her and her lost love from long ago and traced its edges with her fingers, reminiscing about the wonderful life they once shared. Dancing in the rain. Running through the woods together collecting wildflowers. Staying up late into the night to gaze at the stars. They were incredible together—

soulmates, for sure. Their parting had left a void inside her no one could seem to fill. Sure, she had dated other guys, but they didn't compare to *him*. He was the yang to her yin, the other half of her soul.

Had he been looking for her, too? Surely, he must remember the magic they'd shared and the promise they'd made after being forced to lead separate lives. She thought back to the horrible day of the accident. A tear fell from her eye and landed on the picture frame. She stared at it intently until it became a tiny blur.

Willow remembered how they would dance so close she was sure they were only one person. Or all those times he would bring her flowers just because—yellow daisies, her favorite. She would never forget the way he looked at her and made her feel like she was the only woman in the world, and they would be together forever. A love like theirs could never die, could it?

Still, she wondered if he had moved on after they parted. She really couldn't blame him. She had tried it herself a few times.

Yet the thought of him being with someone else hurt her deeply. She had driven down his street a couple of weeks ago and seen him in the arms of pretty blonde. Had he found someone else? Was he happy? Was there still a chance they could rekindle what they once had? Now that she had finally located him, she was eager to pay him a visit, only she knew she would have to take it slow. She couldn't drop in unannounced, especially if another woman now held his heart. It wouldn't be fair to anyone to disrupt their lives.

No, she would wait until the time was right. For

now, she would watch him from a distance. She had to be sure he was ready to see her again. Willow certainly didn't want to ruin their chances of reconciliation. He was far too important to her to risk losing him forever.

She reached into the box and took out the last of the items, her heart-shaped diamond ring. This special heirloom had been passed down for three generations. It was her grandmother's engagement ring, the perfect symbol of undying love. Willow wanted more than anything to find her lost love, no matter what it took. He was her everything, and she regretted that they had spent so much time apart.

Her search had been difficult at first, since she had so little to go on. She had no idea where he'd ended up after the accident. It seemed he'd vanished without a trace. But thanks to an intuitive and a skilled detective, she was able to put together enough clues to lead her to him. Moving nearby was only natural. She had spent enough time out in Armada, on her parents' ten-acre lot with a weathered pole barn and plump farm cats. It was time to move on to something better. Hopefully a life with him.

Willow put her ring on. Maybe it would bring her luck. It had certainly worked for her grandmother. She glanced up at the clock. Two o'clock. He would be home soon, so she would park outside his house and wait. She had to find out if he was seeing the blonde chick. She had to know if it was safe to approach him.

Willow arrived at his house at two fifteen and parked across the street. His car was already home, signaling something was amiss. He always pulled up at two thirty-five. Her face became warm, and her pulse quickened as she thought about what could have happened to him. She hoped he wasn't sick or injured or lying in a hospital bed somewhere. She couldn't bear to see him suffer again. One bad accident was enough. They had already endured their share of struggles and heartbreak. She'd learned long ago that life could certainly be cruel. After all, it had torn apart two soulmates, sending their lives in opposite directions, and claiming them both as its captives. Maybe she should call his house and see if he answered. She couldn't stand the suspense of not knowing why his car was parked outside early while he was nowhere in sight.

She grabbed her cell phone from the console and dialed the number she had memorized but not yet dared to call.

A woman answered after two rings. "Hello?"

Willow contemplated whether or not to ask for him. Was she his girlfriend? Had he gotten home early to spend time with her? Should she pretend to be a telemarketer?

"Hello?" the voice asked again.

Willow breathed deeply and finally mustered up the courage to speak. "Yes, hello. May I please speak to Rob?"

"I'm sorry. You must have the wrong number."

"Oh. So sorry to bother you."

Willow hit the end call button, feeling puzzled. She

had been so sure she had the right number and house. But the woman didn't seem to know who she was talking about. Was she his jealous girlfriend pretending not to know him? How would Willow get to Rob if this woman was always in the way?

CHAPTER 3
SEARCHING

Abundant sunshine and warm tropical breezes held out their arms to greet Chase and his friends in Panama City. Palm trees lined the streets to welcome visitors, and Chase felt like he was part of a giant festive parade of tourists. His buds embraced the lazy, carefree atmosphere and thrived on the sounds of music and laughter echoing through the streets. He, however, was less than enthused.

Despite the hot, bikini-clad chicks who winked at him and flirted, all he could think about was her: the mysterious woman so prominently etched in his mind and soul. He had to find out who she was. Maybe then he would finally understand himself.

He wanted to hang in the hotel room, research dream interpretation, and try to find someone who could help unravel his past, maybe a new therapist or dream analyst. Some time alone would be perfect for a little uninterrupted digging. But his pals had finally talked him into a volleyball game. He didn't want to let them down.

The scratchy sand ground into Chase's bare toes as he walked over to the net. He planted himself in his position, along with his teammates, Joe and Ashley. They had gathered some other teenagers from the beach to join them so the teams were even and full. His friends were pumped up and ready to play. Chase pretended to be stoked and hoped they wouldn't notice he really wasn't.

Ashley served the ball, and Kaitlyn spiked it back to score her team's first point.

"Way to go, Kaitlyn!" Kyle cheered, while Joe cursed.

Kaitlyn puffed her lips out in a duck face and did a happy dance, twirling and flapping her arms around like a chicken. Her fellow players all gave her high fives.

Next, a tall, skinny redhead wearing a black and white polka dot bikini served the ball with a solid whoosh. Chase tried hard to focus on the game. The beach screamed with determined volleyball players, giggling children, squawking seagulls, and the ocean's captivating rush. But they seemed so far away from him now. Although he was physically present, a hazy cloud of separateness invaded his mind, and he drifted to the many questions haunting him.

His friends shouted encouraging words and rooted for their teammates. Energy, laughter, and excitement rang through the beach as the ball traveled swiftly back and forth over the net like a steady pendulum. There was a rhythm and order to everything around him; however, he remained disconnected. He wanted to lie down and melt into the earth, to be a part of something, to feel whole and compete.

Thump.

A sharp pain sliced through his head as the volleyball struck him. He snapped back to reality. Grumbles from his disappointed teammates echoed through the beach. The opposing team hooted and cheered with excitement.

"What the heck, dude?" Joe said. "What's up with you?"

"I'm tired. Think I need a break."

"You seem to be good at taking breaks lately," Kaitlyn said sharply. She sounded annoyed by his lack of participation.

"C'mon, man," Kyle urged. "Don't be a party pooper."

"I think I need some time alone."

"But we didn't go downtown yet," said Ashley. "You've gotta come with us to check it out."

"No, I really don't think—"

"Well, I think…you think too much," Joe uttered, creating an explosion motion around his head with his hands. "Let's wrap up this match and head downtown. It'll be fun. You could use some fun, dude. Right?"

Chase wasn't sure he even knew what fun was anymore and had little interest in traipsing around town. But when he scanned his friends' concerned and pleading faces, only one choice felt comfortable. He folded his arms. "Fine. You win."

☯☯☯

Downtown Panama City bustled with hip restaurants, dynamic office buildings, and shopping. The streets were crowded, and everyone seemed to be in a hurry to get somewhere. It was sensory overload for Chase. He struggled to stay in the moment and keep up with his enthusiastic friends as they ran in and out of shops. The excitement and commotion made him utterly exhausted. It wasn't until he spotted a prominent black and silver business sign that he came back to life. The sign read: Psychic Insights.

Suddenly, Chase found himself alert and curious. He wanted to know more, so he quietly drifted away from his friends to check the establishment out. Silver metallic beads hung in the windows, along with star-shaped decals. As he approached the storefront, he spied a stack of brochures sitting outside the building on the large picture window ledge. He eagerly grabbed one and began reading:

Are you confused? Do you seek answers? Psychic Insights can help. Our experienced and talented intuitives will enlighten you about your past and future. Walk-ins welcome.

Of course! I need to consult a psychic.

He'd always believed there was more to life than the eyes could perceive and had seen evidence that psychic powers were real. Kaitlyn had once told him about her own precognition. Before she moved into the neighborhood, she had a vivid dream of a young, brown-haired boy wearing a red, hooded, Mickey Mouse sweatshirt. When she later met Chase, the boy who lived across the street from her new house, he perfectly matched her dream image and they became instant friends. Coincidence? Not likely. Chase believed he and Kaitlyn were destined to meet, just as he knew deep in his soul he needed to find himself.

He folded the brochure and stuffed it into his pocket. He then ran back to the gift shop where he had last left his friends. Ashley tried on funky, colorful sunglasses while Kaitlyn admired the sparkly jewelry. Joe and Kyle looked bored.

"Where the heck did you go?" Joe asked.

"Checked out an interesting store."

"Cool. What'd ya find?"

"I think I'm gonna see a psychic."

Joe and Kyle looked at each other, and then burst into laughter.

"Good one," Kyle said. He punched Chase playfully in the shoulder.

"Yeah," Joe agreed. "You had me for a minute."

"Guys, I'm serious."

"No way!" exclaimed Kyle.

"You can't tell me you believe in that crap," Joe teased. "I thought you were smart, dude."

"This isn't about smarts. It's about answers. I need to know what's going on with me."

"But a psychic?" asked Kyle. "Are you sure you want to throw away your money on some silly fortune teller?"

"Yeah, man," said Joe. "It's all a scam. They take your money and feed you a bunch of useless voodoo stuff. Besides, you don't need to be psychic to know what's up with you. I can tell you."

"Oh, really? Please do." Chase widened his eyes and shifted his weight to his right leg.

Joe took an exaggerated breath and closed his eyes. He hummed, "Oooommm." He then spoke in a deep, monotonous voice. "I can see what troubles you. It's all so clear to me. You need time alone with your girrrlll."

Kyle wrapped his arms around his sides as he exploded into hysterical fits of laughter. Joe chuckled, too, and they gave each other high fives. Chase turned and began to walk away from them, half-listening to their comments.

"What going on?" Kaitlyn asked.

"Chase wants to see a psychic!" Joe blurted.

"Oh, cool."

"Don't tell me you believe in that crap, too?"

"I think there are some people who have a gift. I've experienced it myself, actually."

"You two are perfect for each other," Joe said. "You're both crazy."

Chiming bells rang loudly through the store as Chase whipped the door open.

"Chase, wait!" Kaitlyn cried.

He turned to look at her.

"Let me come with."

Chase thought about the woman who kept appearing in his head. It wasn't something he wanted to share with Kaitlyn right now. "I'd rather you didn't.

Can't a guy get some privacy once and a while?"

He slammed the door.

Within seconds, Kaitlyn rushed up behind him and grabbed his shoulder. "What's your deal?" she asked.

"No deal. I'm trying to figure stuff out."

"You don't have to do it alone, you know. I can help. I'm your girlfriend, remember? Maybe we should go grab a bite to eat, and we can talk. You know, like old times." She tugged on his arm.

"When's everyone gonna stop telling me what to do?"

"Geesh. What crawled up your butt? We care about you, Chase. We want what's best for you."

"Did it ever occur to you I'm the only one who knows what's best for me?"

"Well, I—"

"I didn't think so. This is something I need to do, Kate. Please try and understand."

"Then let me go with you."

"I'd rather go alone."

"Please. I love psychics. Besides, I need some answers, too." She stared at him with sad, pleading eyes.

A familiar tug of internal conflict rose inside him again. He wanted to say no, but it was so hard for him to think of himself first. He hated disappointing others. All of his life he'd been the agreeable one, rarely arguing and always letting his friends decide where they would go and what they would do. Why did he choose other people's happiness at his own expense?

He sighed. "Okay. Okay. C'mon."

Kaitlyn grabbed his arm and they walked into

Psychic Insights. Soft, New Age music encircled them, along with the calming aroma of lavender and incense. Chase immediately felt welcome.

"Can I help you?" asked a middle-aged woman in an emerald green and gold dress.

"We're here for a psychic reading!" Kaitlyn announced.

"Sure. Follow me. I'll do a couples reading for you. I sense a strong connection between you two."

Chase's heart sank. He'd hoped to dive into his past and find some answers, not have a joint reading with Kaitlyn. Why did she have to interfere?

"Actually," he said. "I'm here to—"

"Of course," the lady said. "I'll have some answers for you. You want to know about the future, right?"

"Well, yes, but I'm also interested in the past."

"You've come to the right place. Please come this way and sit down."

Chase did as he was told. Kaitlyn took a seat next to him, her eyes shining with wonder. She grabbed his hand.

The lady closed her eyes for a minute, breathing in and out slowly. "Yes, I see," she began. "You two are very close. Best friends. Even lovers."

Kaitlyn nodded. Chase felt distracted and glanced around the room at the walls of spiritual and esoteric books. Tarot. Reiki. Chakras. Channeling. Meditation. His eye landed on a section on hypnotherapy. *Was that the solution?* One book in particular intrigued him: *Discover Your Past. Claim Your Future.* Maybe he could buy a copy. He would ask the psychic.

"But something stands in the way of your relationship. I sense…conflict…discord," the psychic continued.

Kaitlyn bobbed her head up and down again.

"The problem is with…him." She pointed at Chase.

He no longer paid attention, wrapped up instead in how he was going to find answers. Who was he really and what held him back?

"Yes," Kaitlyn agreed. "He's going through a rough patch."

"Don't worry, my dear. You will have the relationship you seek."

"Did you hear what she said, Chase?"

"What?"

"Our relationship. We're gonna be okay. I've heard all I need to know."

Chase looked at the psychic, and she gave him a puzzled shrug. Kaitlyn handed the lady her half of the reading fee and rose from her seat.

"C'mon, Chase. Let's go find the others. They'll be happy they were right about us after all."

An unsettled feeling moved across Chase's stomach. *Were they?* "You go ahead. I need some time alone with the psychic."

"You don't want me to stay?"

"No. Please don't be mad."

Kaitlyn looked disappointed, but she didn't insist on staying this time. "Okay." She bounced across the store, past the rows of crystals and incense, and headed out the door.

Once she was out of sight, the psychic looked at

Chase. "You're not sure about your relationship with her, are you?"

"No, ma'am. I'm not."

"I see…It all makes sense."

"What do you mean?"

"I see a female. Pretty brunette."

Chase sat up straighter in his seat. *Could it be the mysterious woman?* "Go on."

"You have a unique bond with her. I feel like this is from another time, another place. Maybe a childhood friend or an ex-girlfriend you want to reconnect with? Or perhaps this is someone you've yet to meet."

"I can't think of anyone specific, but I often dream of a person who fits your description."

"Interesting. I would definitely recommend hypnosis for you. A good therapist should be able to help. You're stuck right now. You need to get things sorted out so you can get on with your future."

"Okay. Sounds like a plan…Um…There's also a book I noticed on your shelf. The blue and white one."

"Yes, about the past?"

"Yep. Can I buy a copy?"

"Why, of course." She scratched the side of her nose, and Chase spotted a tiny emerald jewel, perfectly matched to her dress. This lady definitely fit the part of psychic and resembled a gypsy, complete with sleek black hair, piercing green eyes, and gold hoop earrings.

"What's the book about?"

"It discusses a particular type of hypnosis, one I'm quite fond of, actually. With it, you will explore how the past affects your present and what you can do to release yourself from old baggage. You may have some forgotten memories you need to uncover in order to move forward."

"Awesome. Sounds exactly like what I need."

"Wonderful!" She reached into her desk drawer and pulled out a copy for him. "Did you want me to sign it?"

"Sign it?"

"Yes, I'm the author. I wrote this book."

"Oh, cool. Yes. Please sign it. Thank you."

"You're very welcome." She scribbled an illegible name on the inside cover and handed the book to him. "By the way, there's a spirit here who wants to say something to you."

"Oh?"

"Yes, I'm also a psychic medium. I speak to dead people. There's a gentleman here. Tall, handsome, brown hair—like yours. He says he died in a plane crash."

Chase's stomach churned, and his heart galloped. He pictured his dad's face etched with concern. He fought back tears. "Go on."

"He's telling me something about running away. Running from someone…or something. Do you know what this means?"

"Umm. No, not really."

"Okay. Now he's showing me a police car…some kind of chase. Were you involved in a chase recently?"

"No."

"Hmm. He keeps saying 'chase.' What does it mean?"

"Well, my name is Chase."

Her face lit up, and she pointed a finger. "Yes, that's it! Now he's showing me himself holding a baby boy. Says it's you. He's your father, correct?"

Chase swallowed the growing lump in his throat and nodded. "So what's my dad want to tell me?"

"He says not to give up. The answers you seek will come. Everything you need is already inside you."

"Okay…"

"And he says he loves you and watches over you."

"I love you too, Dad."

"He smiled. He's fading now…getting weaker…Yes, he's gone."

"Anything else?"

She looked off into the distance and nodded. "Your past and your future are not what you think, Chase. Someone or something is definitely in the way of you embracing the person you truly are. You have been very confused lately and need to resolve this conflict in order to be happy. I think you know the truth already. Search within yourself for the answers. It's important for you to take action as soon as possible to discover what could be blocking you."

"Okay."

"Oh, Chase, there is one more thing I want to tell you. The plane crash is significant. It is the key to everything. Trust your intuition on this one. Understand?"

"I think so."

"Very well then. Thanks for stopping in. Love and light to you."

Chase rose from his seat and stumbled. A dizzying

cloud of emptiness tugged at him. He had come to Panama City with his friends, but he couldn't feel more alone. How could he fill the persistent void consuming him? Certainly not here. He had to get out of Panama City, and fast. He sprinted to the city streets in search of a cab. He waved frantically, but no one seemed to notice him. Car after car passed him by or picked up other passengers.

When a yellow cab pulled up across the street, he dashed toward it, only to be met with a blaring horn from an oncoming car. He weaved in and out of stopped traffic, determined to make his escape. By the time he reached his potential ride, the driver had pulled away.

Now what?

CHAPTER 4
INNNER STRUGGLE

Chase reluctantly returned to his hotel room. He still couldn't believe how much trouble he'd had getting a taxi. He wanted to escape this place, but something kept holding him back.

He walked over to the bedside table and picked up a note his friends had left. Joe, Kyle, Kaitlyn, and Ashley were partying in the girls' room. They said they were ordering food—pizza, wings, salad, breadsticks—as well as plenty of beverages. They wanted him to join them when he returned. *Not this time.* He needed to leave Panama City as soon as possible, and no one was there to stop him.

He dialed the airline to find the earliest flight home. "Yes, I need a flight from Panama City to Detroit…tonight."

"I'm sorry, sir. All flights are booked until the day after tomorrow."

"Seriously? There's nothing you can do?"

"No, sir. I'm afraid not. This is our busy season. Spring break and all."

He sighed. "Okay. Thanks anyway."

Chase yawned and set his phone on the nightstand. He knew his friends expected him to join them, and he had no reason not to now, but he really wasn't up for it. Disappointment and exhaustion had set in, and he desperately needed some quiet time to think and regroup.

He removed his shirt and crawled into bed with the book from the psychic in his hands. He might be stuck in Panama City, but at least he could educate himself on hypnosis and therapy. He opened to the first chapter and began reading.

The universe is filled with mysteries, and many are solvable if we look deep within. As a psychic medium, I see clients every day who are sad, angry, afraid, and distraught. Most believe they are stuck and desperately seek closure. One of the most effective techniques I've learned for unraveling the past and embracing the future is regression therapy. This hypnosis technique focuses on resolving past events and traumas that interfere with a person's sense of health and well-being. With a little digging, together the hypnotherapist and the client can uncover forgotten memories. Once these past issues are resolved, the client can lead a better, more fulfilling life.

The concept immediately intrigued him, and he decided he would look up a therapist near his home and give it a try. It certainly couldn't hurt and might finally get him somewhere.

He yawned and stretched. He was too tired to do anything about it right now, but maybe he would have some time tomorrow. He groggily set the book down on the nightstand next to his bed and sank into his pillow.

As he laid there staring at the walls, he drifted into a peaceful slumber where she returned to him—the woman who he felt so much for, but knew so little about. He welcomed her with open arms. At first it was like most of his other visions of her: calm, loving, and full of intrigue. But then the mood shifted, and he drifted to a place he had never been.

The woman took his hand and guided him through the most magnificent garden. He gazed at her, admiring her wavy, flowing brown hair and the way her white sundress showed her body's every curve. Colorful flowers planted throughout the garden surrounded them, emitting a sweet, uplifting scent. They walked together across a stone path, taking in the cheerful chirps of songbirds and the cloudless, vibrant blue sky. The scene had a surreal and magical feel, kind of like what you would expect in a fantasy novel or movie. And Chase was a part of it. He had never felt so happy before.

As he thought about her and the amazing place she had taken him to, he could no longer hold back his feelings. He knew Kyle and Joe would peg him a wuss. An unspoken guy code existed among them: he was supposed to be strong and tough. But in this place, Chase felt anything but strong. He was vulnerable.

The tears slid down his face as the woman led him

toward a white stone fountain and cascading waterfall. Being with her was overwhelming, yet powerful, exhilarating, yet soothing, and he knew right then he could only ever love her.

As they continued down the path to the fountain, Chase saw many white folding chairs set up with people sitting in them, waiting patiently in anticipation. Then he heard music. He immediately recognized the tune as "Canon in D," the song his mother had played over and over on the piano in their living room after his dad died, the song from his parents' wedding day. All at once, it hit him: this was *his* wedding day.

He had never thought much about marriage. His focus was on other things—school, football, studying, choosing a college, and hanging out with girls and his friends. He certainly wasn't ready for adult responsibilities.

But his reluctance went much deeper. He hated seeing his mom suffer without his dad since he died. He never wanted to experience such heartbreak, and fought to protect himself by not getting too close to a girl. Now, in this moment, he was suddenly and unexpectedly faced with images of his wedding day. It was all very odd, and he was puzzled about what had brought him here. Had the visit to the psychic triggered something, a glimpse at the future, maybe?

The guitar music's soothing sounds rang out, and in an instant, Chase and the woman proudly stood in front of the fountain as a waterfall flowed behind them. Chase noticed two doves etched into the fountain's base, along with the words *Love Is Forever.* Something about

Forever gave him chills. Was anything really forever?

The ceremony and vows blurred by at record speed. Then, the woman took Chase's hand and slid a ring onto his finger. He could feel her gentle touch as if he were really there. Something inside him broke free, and he began to sob. He became powerless in her arms as she kissed him tenderly. This gorgeous, loving, mysterious woman was now his wife. He was only seventeen, but in this dream, he felt much older. He was a man about to embark on the journey of his life. He knew what love was, and he was never going to let it go.

A loud voice interrupted his dream. "Dude? Are you awake?" Joe called.

Chase jolted out of his deep sleep and squinted to see his friend. Joe had turned on the lights in their room, and the brightness hurt his eyes.

"What the heck?" Chase asked angrily. "I was sleeping."

"Sorry about the light, dude."

Little did Joe know, the light was not the problem. He had taken Chase away from *her*. Chase wanted so badly to return to the fascinating, magical place where the woman of his dreams lived. Why couldn't she be real?

As usual, Chase fought back the urge to really let Joe have it for interfering in his life once again. But conflict and discord always stressed him out, and he would rather keep peace than see his friend upset. "It's all right," he said. "What's up?"

"It's Kaitlyn."

Chase's heart began to pound. "What happened to

Kaitlyn? Is she okay?"

"Yeah. She's fine. Well, sort of. She's locked herself in the bathroom and is crying. Keeps asking for you."

"Okay. I'll talk to her."

Chase grabbed his shirt from the nightstand, pulled it over his head, and dashed out the door. When he reached Kaitlyn's room, Ashley let him in.

"What's up with Kate?" he asked.

"Don't know." She shrugged. "Joe and I were making out, and she lost it."

"You and Joe?"

She grinned. "Yeah, I've always had a crush on him. Tonight we decided to give things a try. You know, like you and Kaitlyn."

Poor Kaitlyn. He was hardly the model boyfriend lately. He had disappeared on her more than once, and they had only kissed briefly since arriving in Panama City. No wonder she was so upset. She deserved better than he was able to give her right now.

Chase headed for the bathroom and knocked on the door. "Kate? You okay?"

"Go away."

"What's up, babe?"

"Nothing."

"Then why ya crying?"

"Where have you been?" she asked, her voice shaky.

"I stayed a while with the psychic and then went back to my room to rest."

"Was anyone with you?"

"No. Open the door, Kate. This is weird talking through the door."

"Fine," she said, propping it open.

Chase slipped inside before she changed her mind. Kaitlyn perched on the edge of the bathtub. Black mascara smears framed her puffy red eyes, and wads of Kleenex littered the floor. She blew her nose with the intensity of a trombone.

"Why don't you believe I went back to my room to sleep?"

"I don't know. There's this strange tension between us. Almost like you don't really want to be with me. Plus, I noticed all the girls drooling over you today. I thought maybe you decided to hang out with one of them."

"I would never betray you."

"Yeah. Whatever. All guys say it, but do they really mean it?"

"Hey now, don't be comparing me to other guys."

"Well, then, why aren't you spending time with me tonight?"

"I'm tired. I have a lot on my mind."

"I feel like I'm losing you, Chase. Each day you drift farther and farther away. Are you sure there's nothing else? No other girl? No one who's caught your eye?"

An image of Chase's dream woman came to his mind. He cleared his throat. Technically, there was somebody else. But how could he tell Kaitlyn he was in love with someone he had never met? How could he explain another girl was on his mind and in his dreams, but he had no idea who she was?

"I want the truth, Chase. Is there somebody else?"

"I'm not dating anyone else."

"But you want to."

"No, I don't."

"You're lying. I can hear it in your voice."

"Not exactly."

Guilt rose within him like a high tide. At any moment, it would crash against the shore and wash away the solid friendship they'd once had. As hard as it was, he needed to tell Kaitlyn how he really felt. She deserved to know the truth.

"What do you mean?" She grabbed his hand and looked into his eyes. "You can tell me anything."

"I'm not sure about us being a couple. It doesn't feel right to me."

"So what are you saying?"

"I'm saying I value our friendship and think it'd be best if we took a break from this whole couple thing. Ya know, until I sort things out. I feel so confused lately, Kate. I don't even know who I am. It's not fair to you."

A worried look came over her face, but she still nodded, tears gently streaming down her cheeks.

"You're not mad?" Chase asked.

"No." She looked down and picked at her nails. "It hurts, but I could never be mad at you. I will miss you, Chase."

"No you won't. We're buds, remember? BFFs. Nothing can ever come between us."

"Nothing," she agreed. "Now let's get out of the bathroom. This is weirding me out."

"Good point."

They ran out of the bathroom before anyone wondered what they were doing. The gang sat waiting on the couch with their swimsuits on.

"There they are," Joe said. "Did you kiss and make up?"

Kate folded her arms and looked away. "I'd rather not talk about it."

"It's okay, Kate," said Ashley. "We can talk later. Whenever you're ready."

"Yeah. Besides, we have better things to do. We're all going for a late night swim," Kyle said. "Thought you two could join us."

Chase groaned. "I'm not sure I'm up for a swim right now." He looked at Kaitlyn.

She nodded, giving her approval for him to join them.

"You not up for much of anything lately," Joe said. "C'mon, it won't be the same without you."

Kaitlyn let out a tiny squeak. She sniffed and turned for the bathroom. Chase thought she was about to burst into tears, but she managed to keep it together.

"I'll get my suit on," she said quietly as she headed for the bathroom.

Joe looked back at Chase. "Well, dude, are you coming, or what?"

Chase's heart began to pound as guilt sunk its fierce claws into him. There really was no escape. If he stayed here, everyone would be disappointed, and he would feel bad. If he went, he would be forced to endure an evening of unwanted shenanigans and uncomfortable tension between him and Kaitlyn. He knew she was devastated about their breakup. But guilt was more powerful than discomfort, so he went with the latter.

"Fine. Gimme a sec to change."

"You bet. We'll wait in the hallway."

Chase darted to his room and changed quickly into his red and white swim trunks. He snatched a crisp white towel hanging from the bar and met Joe and the gang in the hallway outside his room.

"We're gonna have a blast!" Joe shouted. He grabbed Ashley and wrapped his arms around her.

"Shhh," said Ashley. "Some people are probably sleeping."

Kaitlyn looked at Chase and turned away without saying a word. She was obviously heartbroken, and he hated being the cause of her hurt. His change of heart about their relationship likely made no sense to her. Someday, he would explain. He would tell her about the beautiful twenty-something brunette who held his heart. Someone he had never even met, but who felt so real to him. He needed Kaitlyn to understand it wasn't anything she'd done wrong. For now, he would spare her any added pain.

"C'mon, let's go," said Kyle.

They all ran down the hotel hallway to the nearest exit. As they flung open the doors and headed into the warm, humid spring air, a jet engine roared above Chase's head and caught his attention. All at once, the airplane catastrophe replayed again in his mind: the shaking plane, the pilot's alarming announcement, the billowy smoke, and the overwhelming feelings of dread.

By the time they reached the beach, fiery images had killed Chase's self-sacrificing mood. He no longer felt a strong desire to please his friends. Fear, sadness, and panic now replaced his concern for others. He watched helplessly as the flames engulfed the plane and the smoke did its familiar tantalizing waltz, swallowing him up like a giant whale. He gripped the plane seat with all his might and braced himself for the impact of the plane as it hit the ground. But before it did, he turned his head to the left to look at the passenger sitting next to him. He gasped. It was her, the woman from his dreams!

Chase's head became dizzy and lightheaded; his breathing was erratic. As the plane struck the ground, he let out a horrible scream and fell face-down in the sand.

CHAPTER 5
PIECE OF THE PUZZLE

Chase emerged from the blackness when a familiar girl's voice called to him. It sounded like the distant buzz of an insect, but with a more urgent tone. Slowly, he slipped back into consciousness.

"Chase? Chase? Are you okay? Answer me, please."

He struggled to speak, not quite sure where he was or what was going on. "Darla?"

"No. It's Kaitlyn. Who's Darla?"

Chase rubbed his sore head and opened his eyes, slowly focusing on the fuzzy image in front of him. Kaitlyn leaned over him. She stroked his forehead while Joe and Kyle stood on either side of her. Ashley cried nearby. They all stared at him like he had come back from the dead. He sort of felt as if he had.

"What the heck happened?" he asked.

"You looked pale. Then you screamed and fell to

the ground," Kaitlyn said. "Are you all right?"

He sat up slowly and brushed the sand off his body. The ground beneath him was hard and cold even though he sat in soft, damp sand. His eyes darted across his environment, taking in the shaky images of his friends and the dark, shadowy beach. He felt a little unsteady, so he leaned his head on Kaitlyn's shoulder.

Currents of panic rolled through him. Although his whole body now trembled, the ocean waves crashed against the shore and provided some comfort. He'd always found the ocean's roar soothing, and tonight was no exception.

Adding to his sense of security were his concerned and sympathetic friends. He was so relieved they were with him, because he certainly didn't want to be alone now. An uneasy sensation of fear and dread still lurked below the surface, but he couldn't remember what had provoked his screams or had made him fall. His head was dizzy with emotion and confusion, and he knew something profound had happened. But what?

"Dude, you don't look so good," Joe said. "Maybe we'd better get some help."

"Good idea," agreed Kyle.

"No, I'm fine." Chase cleared his throat and breathed in the salty ocean air. It calmed him a bit.

"Sorry, dude, we're not taking any chances. I'll get the security guard."

"Whatever. But really, man, I'm fine."

Kyle hurried off to the hotel for help, while Chase continued to reorient himself. He looked at Kaitlyn and managed a small smile.

"Oh, Chase! I'm so glad you're okay," Kaitlyn gushed. "Can I get you anything?"

"Maybe some water."

"You've got it! Ash, can you keep an eye on him while I go to the vending machine? I think I saw one on the second floor."

"Sure thing," Ashley said, wiping stray tears from her eyes. She wrapped her towel around him.

"Thanks, Ash."

"No prob."

About ten minutes later, Chase spotted a skinny young guy coming toward him. Scraggly, sand-colored hair hung down his neck like a surfer dude or lifeguard. It was Kyle. Chase had never noticed how well Kyle fit in here. Two other people accompanied his friend: a security guard and another tall, serious man.

"Hello," the guard said. "I'm Ricco, hotel security supervisor." He extended his hand and clasped Chase's sweaty palm in a firm handshake.

Ricco was a husky dude with curly black hair. His expression was stern but compassionate. He wore a neatly pressed navy blue uniform that screamed authority. "And this is Dr. Finch," he continued. "He works at the medical clinic across the street. They were closing up for the night, and he agreed to come check you out."

"Hello," said Dr. Finch in a soft-spoken voice. He shook Chase's hand with a delicate, almost feminine touch to match his calming demeanor. He wore a simple Hawaiian shirt and tan pants.

"Thanks for coming," Chase said, as Dr. Finch

pulled out his stethoscope. He listened to Chase's heartbeat and had him take some deep breaths.

"Your heart sounds good." He nodded approvingly. "Now let's check your blood pressure." He placed the cuff around Chase's arm and pumped it up. After a few minutes, he nodded again. "128 over 72."

He then looked in Chase's eyes, ears, nose, and throat. "Very good," he said, putting away his equipment. "Your friend told me what happened. From the sound of it, I think you had a panic attack. Everything seems okay now. Take it easy and get some rest."

"Okay," Chase agreed. "Thank you, Doctor."

"You're welcome. It was nice to meet you. If you have any problems, please be sure to come to our walk-in urgent care clinic. Now, you kids stay safe, okay?"

"You bet," Chase answered.

Ricco and Dr. Finch headed back to the hotel. Chase breathed a sigh of relief.

"Dude, you scared the heck out of us." Joe patted Chase on the back. "We thought you were having a heart attack or something. Does this happen to you often?"

"I have a lot of panic attacks."

"What about falling down and passing out?" Joe asked.

"That's a new one. I probably hyperventilated."

"Do you call out strange girls' names often?" Ashley asked.

"What are you talking about?"

Joe chuckled and elbowed Ashley. "Yeah. Did you see the look on Kaitlyn's face when Chase called out some other girl's name? She was pissed."

"Shhh," Ashley said, raising a finger to her lips. "Here comes Kaitlyn."

Kaitlyn walked up to the gang and handed Chase a bottle of water. "Here, babe."

"Thanks, Kate. What would I do without you?"

"Good question," Kaitlyn said, her voice becoming sharp.

"What do you mean?"

"You know darn well what I mean. Let's be honest, Chase. You were cheating on me! Why else would you dump me?"

"What?" Joe ran his hands through his curly black hair. "You two broke up? Did I miss something?"

"Apparently we all did," said Kyle, putting his arm around Kaitlyn.

"Yeah, guys," Ashley chimed in. "Please tell us: What's going on?"

"You tell them." Kaitlyn folded her arms and looked away.

"Kate, I really have no idea what you're talking about," Chase insisted.

"Really? So are you going to tell me who Darla is then?"

"Who?"

"Darla."

"I have no idea. I don't even know any Darlas."

"Well, you called out her name," Kaitlyn said, putting a hand on her hip. "After you came to."

Chase choked on his water. "I did? Must have been confused or something." *Who the heck is Darla?*

The name evoked a strange, tingly sensation throughout his body, but he couldn't think of anyone named Darla. Deep inside, he knew it must mean something. But what? He would have to explore all of this when he felt up to it.

"None of this is important right now," Kyle said. He was always the calm one. "Let's get you back to the hotel. We can talk later." He grabbed Chase's hand and pulled him up.

"Good idea," Chase agreed. "Thanks, man." His head now pounded, and he could taste sand in his mouth.

Kyle put Chase's arm around his shoulder, and Joe did the same. Together, they escorted him back to his room. No one said a word, but it was clear they had one thing on their minds: making sure Chase was safe.
Despite their efforts, Chase knew the truth. He was never really safe. His past still haunted him, and his gut told him something was very wrong with his life. But what?

☯☯☯

The next morning, Chase awoke to sunshine peering in through the leaf-print curtains of their hotel room. Joe slept soundly in the bed next to Chase, covers tossed about in a chaotic mess. His T-shirt rode up a bit and gave a peek at his slightly chubby belly underneath. He let out a robust snore.

A girl's giggle came from the brown microfiber couch on the other side of the room.

Chase rubbed the sleep out of his eyes and peered in

the direction of the sound. "Kaitlyn? What are you doing here?"

"I was really worried about you. So I slept on the couch."

"You didn't have to. But thanks." Once again, Kaitlyn had proven she cared about more than herself.

"You're welcome. That's what friends are for. We are still friends, right?"

"Of course we are. Did you sleep much?"

"Not really. I was too busy keeping an eye on you. How are you feeling today?"

"Better."

A stray tear trickled down Kaitlyn's cheek. "Good," she said, her voice cracking. "I don't want to lose you."

"Never." Chase wondered exactly how deep her feelings for him ran. "Kate? You okay?"

"Yeah." She sat up and smoothed her hot pink, zebra pajama top. "Can we go out on the balcony and talk?"

"Sure."

Chase took her hand, and they headed out there. The balcony overlooked the Gulf of Mexico, offering stunning views and a breathtaking breeze. It was the closest to paradise Chase had ever been, with the exception of his recent dream.

He and Kaitlyn sat on the two white, plastic beach chairs and gazed out into the sparkling blue waters. The sun glistened across the ocean in shimmering sparkles. Seagulls cawed overhead while a few scattered guests walked along the water's edge, some hand in hand. Kaitlyn put her head on his shoulder and held his hand.

"Chase, this is really hard for me. You know, not being a couple."

"I know. I'm sorry."

"I really want you back." She leaned in and kissed him tenderly.

The sounds and sights of the beach faded, and Chase found himself sitting on a blanket in a park, making out with his dream girl. They were nestled amid the trees on a picture-perfect day with bright blue skies, fluffy white clouds, and abundant sunshine. A picnic basket sat nearby, as did a half-empty bottle of lemonade. A slight wind gently blew the leaves of the trees back and forth. The breeze refreshed him, and his whole being came to life as they kissed. He gently pushed her down on the blanket and the kissing escalated. "Oh, Darla," he cried.

She pulled abruptly away from him. Chase opened his eyes to see Kaitlyn staring back at him angrily, tears streaming down her face.

"No. No. Kate. It's not what you think."

"Stop lying to me, Chase. I know there's someone else. Please tell me who the heck Darla is."

As much as Chase preferred to keep his dream girl to himself, he needed to tell Kaitlyn. She had the wrong idea and deserved the truth. He took a deep breath and sighed. "Earlier, when I said I didn't know any Darlas, I meant it. But now I think I might know who she is."

"Oh?"

"You know how I've been having those visions all these years."

"Yes, of the awful plane crash."

"Well, there's more."

"Do tell."

"I've also had dreams of a woman."

"What woman? Do I know her?" Kaitlyn folded her arms and looked away.

"No. I've never seen or met her. I don't even know her name. She may not even be real."

"How strange."

"Yes, it is. But the weirdest thing…in my dreams, I'm in love with her."

Kaitlyn sighed and rolled her eyes at him. "Seriously? You're in love with some fantasy woman? You traded me for a figment of your imagination? You can't be serious!"

"I am. I feel like I know her, like I've always known her. And now I believe her name may be Darla."

Kaitlyn groaned and put her head in her hands. Then she began to cry. "Your dreams can only mean one thing," she said sadly. "They're premonitions of the future. The psychic wasn't talking about us when she said I would have the relationship I seek. We're really not supposed to be together after all."

"You don't know what's meant to be." He grabbed her hand and stroked the back of it with his thumb.

"Yes, I do," she objected, pulling her hand away. "Why do you think I cried last night? When you didn't join us for pizza and snacks, I realized there's something standing in the way of us being a couple. We're together, but not *really* together. It all makes sense now."

"I'm sorry, Kate. I never meant to hurt you."

"I can't believe I found my dream guy, and he's off

dreaming about someone else. Someone who doesn't even exist yet."

"She's real to me. And I hope to find her someday. I'm sorry if that upsets you."

"It does…a lot...You have no idea how much it hurts…" She hung her head. "But I know you can't control how you feel. I can't make you love me."

"True. But I don't want to lose you as a friend either."

She folded her arms and pouted. "You haven't lost me. I'm still here."

"Good."

They both let out a big sigh and looked out at the gorgeous scenery beckoning them. Chase's eyes fixed on a royal blue sailboat gliding gently through the water. It traveled effortlessly across the waves. He wished life were so carefree and easy. "What now?" he asked.

Kaitlyn shrugged. "I really don't know. Do you want to go down to the restaurant and get some breakfast?"

"Sure. But lemme grab a quick shower first."

"Okay. I'll go back to my room and do the same. Meet you down there in half an hour?"

"You bet."

☯☯☯

When Kaitlyn joined Chase for breakfast, he noticed her eyes were still puffy and her face was red. He felt terrible to be the source of her suffering. He hoped, in time, they would be able to mend their friendship and go back to the way things once were. If there was one thing Chase knew about himself: he hated conflict and tried hard to keep peace, no matter what.

Chase and Kaitlyn munched on Belgian waffles with fresh strawberries and a side of bacon. Chase hadn't realized how hungry he was until he began eating. As he scarfed down his food, Kaitlyn bombarded him with questions.

"So what exactly happened out there on the beach last night?"

Chase thought hard for a few minutes in an attempt to remember. He recalled how they were all heading to the beach for an evening swim. What happened next? He heard a noise and looked up into the sky…Oh, yes! An airplane cruised overhead.

His throat tightened, and suddenly everything came back to him. He remembered his plane crash vision and how he had seen her, the girl in his dreams, sitting next to him as the plane went down. What a shocker! Kaitlyn claimed he had called out a name, Darla. Was her name actually Darla, or had he made it up? Could his dream woman really exist somehow, somewhere?

"I had another one of my visions."

"I know. But there was more, wasn't there?"

"Yes."

"What else?"

"You know, I fell down in the sand and passed out."

"But why?" she prodded, like a child full of curiosity.

"I saw details of the plane crash. It was awful."

"But you've seen the crash many times before, and

it never made you fall or pass out."

"True."

"Then what was different this time?"

"She was there."

"Who? Your dream woman?"

"Yep."

"She died in a plane crash with you?"

"Yes. And it scared the crap out of me!"

"Oh, Chase, this is so sad. If she is a part of your future, then…"

"I know. I thought the same thing."

They were both quiet for a bit. Chase pondered the possibility of meeting the woman of his dreams someday, getting married, and then dying tragically in a plane crash. Maybe they were heading off on their honeymoon? Or a trip away from the children? Oh, Lord, what if they had kids and were forced to leave them behind? What a horrible scenario!

If this was his future, then Chase wanted no part of it. If he ever did meet this woman, he would steer clear of her. But perhaps the future could be altered if he made different choices. He was determined to prevent the airplane catastrophe, even if it meant never building a life with the woman he loved.

Kaitlyn grabbed his hand across the table and gave it a reassuring squeeze. "We still don't know for sure if the visions are of your future. Maybe something from your childhood is tripping you up and causing you to have these weird fantasies. I know your dad died in a plane crash. Maybe someone was with him. The woman could have been another passenger. You know, like a relative, family friend, or co-worker or something. Or you could have had a scary airplane trip or close call before your dad died. You were so little. Maybe you don't remember everything. The romantic dreams with the woman could be a coping mechanism or something."

"Hmm. Could be," he said, feeling more hopeful. "I'll have to ask my mom more about the crash when we get home."

"Hey!" Joe called from the restaurant doorway. He wore a green T-shirt and colorful, Hawaiian-print shorts. "You two snuck out for breakfast without me." He patted his belly.

"Sorry, man," Chase said. "You were still sleeping, and we were hungry."

"You were too busy snoring." Kaitlyn laughed. Her face had brightened, and she didn't look quite so forlorn.

Chase knew she was trying hard to hide her feelings.

"I don't snore," Joe protested.

"You're right," Chase said. "Sounds more like a bear growling."

They all chuckled as Joe pulled up a seat to join them. Kyle and Ashley followed shortly after, and they discussed their plans for their last day in Panama City.

"Let's go to Shipwreck Island Waterpark," suggested Ashley.

"Nah, I think I'm getting waterlogged," Joe said.

"What about St. Andrews State Park?" asked Kyle. "I hear the scenery there is awesome, and they have two fishing piers if we want to fish. Though we'll have to stop and grab a license somewhere."

"No way am I touching a slimy worm or fish," said Kaitlyn with a frown. "I might mess up my nails or catch a disease. Count me out."

"You're such a diva, Kate," teased Ashley.

"You know it. I've got to stay beautiful for the guys. I'm single now." She batted her baby blue eyes and tossed her blonde hair around. But beneath her playful exterior was a deep sadness. Chase could see it.

"Oh, Lord," moaned Joe.

"I have an idea," Chase said, changing the subject. "Why don't we go to Gulf World Marine Park? We can check out the sea lions, stingrays, reptiles, and tropical birds. And you can even swim with a dolphin if you want."

"Sounds cool," said Joe. "Who votes for the marine park?"

They all raised their hands.

"It's settled then," Kyle said. "We'll go there. We can rent a car so we can bum around town after. Let's finish our breakfast so we can get started."

"But wait," said Ashley. "There's something we need to do first."

"Oh?" Chase asked.

She smiled and winked an eye at them. "A toast," she said, raising her glass of orange juice. "To good times and great friends."

" Here, here!" Joe shouted.

An elderly couple at a nearby table gawked at them.

They all raised their glasses and clinked them together. Kyle clinked his a bit too hard and spilled juice on the table. They all cheered. The girls giggled, and

Chase and Joe gave Kyle a hard time.

"What is wrong with today's youth?" Chase overheard the old lady say, which sent them all into a burst of hysterical laughter.

"Ready to get out of here?" Joe asked.

Chase glanced at his cell phone. It was after nine o'clock. He still wanted to do some research and find a therapist. "I'll catch up with you guys later. There's something I need to take care of first."

Kaitlyn rolled her eyes, and Joe groaned. Chase ignored them for a change and headed for the door, eager for some answers.

"We'll wait here. If you're not back in thirty minutes, we're coming to get you," Joe said.

☯☯☯

Chase settled into a comfortable, burgundy, plush chair in the corner of his hotel room with his laptop. The curtains were drawn, creating a much-needed atmosphere of privacy and seclusion, both of which were hard to come by in such a lively city with a bunch of high-strung teenagers. He needed these quiet, precious moments to begin his search for a good therapist who might be able to help him finally find himself. He typed "Michigan therapists hypnosis" into the Google search engine and eagerly scanned the results.

One result in particular caught his attention. *Recall past trauma. Reclaim your life. Specializing in hypnosis and psychotherapy. Justine Echoson, Chesterfield, Michigan.*

On instinct, Chase quickly grabbed his cell phone off the small table next to him and dialed the number.

A friendly lady answered.

"I'd like to make an appointment with Justine…yes, Saturday at ten would be fine."

After giving his information, Chase opened the curtains and peered out into the sunlight. The Gulf of Mexico's clear blue waters seemed more inviting than he had noticed, and he felt hopeful, even energized. He slid open the balcony door and stepped outside to breathe in the salty ocean air. He was on a mission now. He was determined to unlock the secrets of his psyche. This time, nothing or no one would stand in his way.

"This is what you ditched us for?" Joe called out from behind him.

"No, I did some research and made an important phone call."

"Sounds serious."

"Yes, Joe. It is. I made an appointment with a hypnotherapist."

Joe laughed. "I'm sorry, dude. You crack me up! You're usually so smart and sensible. What's gotten into you? First a crazy psychic, and now this?"

"It's not funny. I need to do something to figure out what's up with me."

"Your dad died in a plane crash. It freaked you out. You don't need some quack to tell you what you already know. If you ask me, I think you need to lighten up and relax."

"I can't just 'lighten up.' My gut's telling me I need to get to the bottom of stuff."

"Well, I hate to break it to you, dude. Your brain isn't in your gut; it's in your head. You'd better start using it, otherwise everyone's gonna think you're insane."

"I've given this a lot of thought, Joe. I need to do this."

"Like you needed to dump Kaitlyn? What were you thinking, man? You had a good thing with her, and you blew it. Don't throw your life away by chasing after stuff that doesn't matter. Get your priorities straight before you get yourself into trouble."

"I'm already in trouble. I feel like I'm drowning, and if I don't figure out how to stay afloat, my life will be over."

A knock on the glass door interrupted their conversation. Chase gritted his teeth and clenched his hands. Everyone seemed to think they knew what was best for him, only most of the time they were wrong.

"Hey, guys, we going out, or what?" asked Kyle

"Chase thinks being hypnotized will solve all his problems. He's even got an appointment." Joe chuckled.

Kyle raised his eyebrows and looked at Chase. "You've got to be kidding me!"

"No joke," Chase said.

"You don't need a hypnotherapist," Kyle said. "You need to stop being so intense and have fun. Everyone else is, why can't you?"

Chase often wondered the reason himself. Why couldn't he let loose and have a good time? It sounded simple enough, but he was caught in a complex web of emotion and uncertainty. Until he solved the puzzle of who he was and what he wanted, he would never rest. It was time to find himself.

CHAPTER 6
MISSING

Willow hadn't seen Rob lately. She'd gone by his house twice and watched for him. Where was he?

She imagined the blonde girl now kept tabs on him. His girlfriend probably hadn't liked when she called for him the other day. If only she knew the love he'd once shared with Willow. His girlfriend would either cling tightly for fear of losing him or give up, knowing she could never compete.

Willow had to find a way to approach him. Once he saw her and realized who she was, nothing would stand in their way. They would be together again.

The doorbell rang and jolted Willow from her seat. She peeked out the window and smiled. Max had come! Max had been a good friend of her mother's. They had met in college and stayed in touch, despite her father's jealousy. After Willow's mother passed, Max had taken it upon himself to look after her like a surrogate dad. She appreciated him checking up on her from time to time, especially since she no longer had a father figure in her life. She had also recently asked him to help her find Rob. Maybe he had some news.

"Hey, pumpkin. How are you doing?"

"Okay, Max. It's still hard for me...you know, without Mom."

"I know, sweetie. So many times I wanted to take your mom away from your father. I knew he was trouble. I'm so sorry for all you've been through."

"I'll survive. Having Rob back in my life will make all the difference. So, any new information? Do you know where he's been lately? Is he dating the blonde chick?"

"I'm sorry, Willow."

Her heart sank as she pictured Rob and the beautiful blonde kissing and holding each other. She longed to feel his lips on hers again, to run her hands across his soft skin, to smell his aftershave. From the very depths of her soul, she ached to be with him.

"The woman I saw is his girlfriend then, right?"

"No. The information you gave me was a dead end. There is no one with the name Rob at the address you have."

"Really? I was so sure.... So the lady on the phone actually didn't know who I was talking about?"

"Yep. Are you sure it was Rob you saw outside the house?"

"Yes...I mean, I think so...I guess I can't be sure."

"What made you think Rob lived there?"

"A psychic. She gave me a street name and said it was Rob's. And then when I waited outside his house…I swear it was him."

"I hate to break this to you, dear, but I believe you were the unfortunate victim of a scam. I know how badly you want to find Rob. I think you are so desperate that everyone is starting to look like him. Take some time. Get some rest. You really need a break, Willow. You've been through so much. Call me if you have any new information, and I'll help you locate him. Okay?"

"Okay. Thanks."

Max gave her a reassuring hug and returned to his car. As Willow watched him drive away, a tear slid down her cheek, and a lonely ache penetrated her heart. She'd been so sure she had found Rob. If the guy she'd seen wasn't him, then where was he?

CHAPTER 7
UNCERTAIN FUTURE

The bright blue sky greeted Chase and his friends as they got into the car to enjoy their last day of spring break. Joe had recently turned 18, so he had rented a red Camaro convertible. They were all excited to take it for a spin and check out some sites. Chase put on his happy face and pretended to be enthused for his friends' sake. In truth, he really wanted to get back home and have his appointment with the hypnotherapist.

Kyle and Joe were in the front seat, and Chase sat in the back between Kaitlyn and Ashley. As they headed to Gulf World Marine Park, the girls applied makeup and tried to keep their hair from getting too wild. Ashley was the lucky one. Her light brown, shoulder-length hair was straight and simple, so it wasn't easily messed up. Kaitlyn, on the other hand, struggled to keep her perfectly styled, curly blonde mop in check.

Chase found it quite entertaining, the way girls

always cared so much about how they looked. Obviously, they had no idea guys didn't give a crap about makeup or the latest hairstyles. Most guys saw through girls' painted exteriors to their real beauty, and often, the chicks who fussed little were the sexiest and most appealing. There was nothing more irresistible than a girl who looked naturally beautiful. Chase was certain every teenage guy out there noticed someone like that.

Still oblivious, Kaitlyn and Ashley chatted about which shade of lipstick looked best while Kyle and Joe talked about their day and the sites they would soon see. Chase remained deep in his thoughts about what made girls attractive. He knew his mystery woman wasn't just a beautiful face. There was something truly special about her. Her beauty came from the inside. A radiant light emanated from her soul and found its way to his heart. Every time he dreamed of her, she cast her spell on him, and he was powerless to escape her clutches.

"You're pretty quiet," Ashley said. "Whatcha thinking about?"

Chase shrugged. "Girls."

"Oh yeah, baby," Joe bellowed.

Ashley rolled her eyes. "Figures. Typical guy."

Kaitlyn shot Chase an angry glance. "I thought you weren't interested in girls. Except for your dream woman."

"Doesn't mean I don't notice sometimes."

"Yep," agreed Joe. "Who wouldn't appreciate a hot chick? And there's plenty of them here."

"What dream woman?" asked Ashley.

"It's nothing really," Chase lied.

"Chase has been having dreams about some beautiful woman. Thinks he might meet her someday," Kaitlyn offered.

"Nothing wrong with dreaming about a beautiful woman," said Joe. "I once had a dream some amazon chick from the jungle threw a rope around me and lured me in. It was really hot."

"Aren't we hot enough for you?" Kaitlyn quipped.

Deep down, Chase knew she was serious. She was still bothered by the fact their relationship was truly over.

"This has nothing to do with looks," Chase said. "My dreams feel like a glimpse into the future or something. I really feel like I know this woman."

"I felt like I knew the amazon chick, too," said Joe. "Her name was Wilma. She was a sexy redhead with a large animal bone in her hair."

"Oh em gee." Ashley laughed. "You're thinking of the old cartoon show, *The Flintstones*."

"Oh…I thought she seemed familiar." Joe's face turned red as he chuckled. "See, Chase, your girl probably isn't real either. My guess is you saw her in some movie on HBO. All the good-looking chicks are on TV."

"What did the psychic say about all of this?" Kaitlyn asked.

"Don't tell me you're still hung up on this psychic stuff," Kyle grumbled.

"Actually, she seemed to have pretty good insight," said Chase. "She saw a woman who looked like the person in my dreams. Thinks she might be an old childhood friend or future girlfriend."

Sadness spread across Kaitlyn's face, and she nervously searched her purse for her sunglasses. She put them on and looked off in the distance.

"Kate," Chase said, putting his hand on hers. "Please don't be upset. You know how I feel about you. You're an amazing girl, and I'm very lucky to call you my friend. The right guy's out there for you."

"Chase is right," Ashley agreed. "When we get back, I'll set you up with my friend, Trevor. He's a cutie."

Kaitlyn squeezed Chase's hand. "I'm sorry. Not having you as my boyfriend is going to take some getting used to."

"I know. For me, too."

Kaitlyn leaned her head on Chase's shoulder.

"Friends forever," Chase whispered.

"Yes," she agreed.

The convertible coasted along the streets of Panama City. Chase relished the feel of the wind on his skin while Kyle drove, and Joe flipped through the radio channels, trying to find the perfect tune. He finally decided on "Don't Let Me Down" by The Chainsmokers.

"Oooh!" exclaimed Ashley. "Turn it up. I love this song!"

Kaitlyn agreed, and they both began singing loudly and off-key.

Chase snickered. It was great to be among good friends. Even though they could be annoying and persistent sometimes, they made life interesting and less stressful. Chase thought about how much he would miss these guys when they all went away to college. He had known most of them since kindergarten, so it was weird to think about not hanging out or seeing each other anymore.

"Hey, Chase," Ashley said. "You're pretty quiet again. What's up?"

"Thinking about college."

"You're going to State, right?"

Chase had planned to go to Michigan State University on a football scholarship to study chemistry. His high school science teacher had urged him to do so because of his exceptional grades, and his mother approved. Joe had also chosen State and often remarked at what a great time they would have as college buddies. So it seemed like the right choice. Only now, he wasn't so sure.

"Yeah, I think. I don't know. I haven't made up my mind yet."

"Dude, we're supposed to room together," said Joe. "Don't bail on me now."

"What do you mean you don't know? You have a full scholarship. You have to go," Ashley urged.

Did he? The tug to forge his own path pulled hard on him. A whole world lay before him, waiting to be explored. Wasn't becoming an adult about finding himself? Or was he forced to keep his innermost desires hidden and unacknowledged to avoid conflict with those he cared about? The struggle was real, and it ate him up inside.

Chase shrugged. "Yeah, I guess."

"Don't think about college," Joe said. "It's depressing. Live for the moment."

"Yeah," said Kaitlyn. "We'll have plenty of time to think about the future later. I'm sure you'll make the right choice."

Future. The mention of it caused Chase's heart to beat faster. He really wasn't sure what the future held for him. Still, he couldn't shake the feeling his life was about to change in a big way. He needed to get back home so he could get started.

CHAPTER 8
DEAD END

The delicious aroma of fresh garlic and basil greeted Chase as he opened the door to the red brick ranch house he had lived in since he was five. He and his parents had shared many good memories there, including pillow fights, family game nights, and leaf raking marathons. Chase had loved to play Uno, maybe because he always won. But some of their best times had been when they gathered around the country oak table for conversation and a good home-cooked meal. Mom could make a mean pasta dinner and knew it was Chase's favorite dish.

She was at the kitchen stove cooking spaghetti sauce when he walked in with his suitcase. Her graying brown hair was pulled back in a bun, and she wore her favorite Levi jeans and an old yellow T-shirt.

"Oh, Chase," she cried. "I missed you so much, honey." She threw her arms around him and planted a kiss on his cheek.

"I missed you too, Mom." He set his suitcase down and took his place at the kitchen table.

"How was your trip, sweetie?"

"Good. It was good." He thought of the enchanting garden where he'd married his dream girl, and the way she'd kissed him. A smile spread across his face. Being with her was worth any risk. He needed to find her.

"I'm glad. You do look a little sunburned, though. You have to be careful in the sun, you know. You really need to wear more sunscreen."

"I know, Mom."

"You'll be going off to college soon, so you need to make sure you take care of yourself properly."

There it was again. His friends were all counting on him to go to State and study chemistry, and so was his mom. If he didn't go, he'd disappoint a lot of people and risk shattering his long-time friendships. College seemed like a reasonable plan.

But Chase felt far from reasonable right now. Deep inside him, a fire burned. Once a spark, it had become increasingly stronger as graduation drew near. He could no longer ignore it.

"Yeah. I'm not so sure about college anymore."

"What? You were excited about going. And you and Joe were looking forward to rooming together. What happened?"

"I don't know if it's the right choice for me."

"Oh, honey. It's normal to have doubts. Growing up is a big deal. But you'll have a good friend with you. You'll be okay."

"It's not about growing up, Mom. Lately, I feel…so lost."

"Well, don't throw your future away because of it. You've worked hard, Chase. You deserve to go to a good college and land the career of your dreams."

Mom had a point. The only problem: college and a career in chemistry wasn't his dream. It was hers. It was theirs—his friends' and teachers'. He didn't even know what he wanted because he'd spent his whole life listening to and accommodating others. He needed to find himself now. His life and his future depended on it.

He thought again of Darla, his disturbing plane crash visions, and the many questions flooding his mind. He had passed out on spring break when he saw an image of Darla and him on a doomed plane. He had called out her name without even realizing it or knowing who she was. All of these thoughts and images had to mean something. He had to take action to find out what.

"Mom, can I ask you something?"

Mom poured the box of noodles into the boiling water and then stirred the sauce again. "Sure, sweetie."

"Before Dad died, were there any close calls? Was I ever in a plane when something happened, like an emergency landing?"

"Well, let me think…Your dad had a couple of minor plane crashes in his private plane, but no one was hurt. You weren't there for those. Oh, wait…I almost forgot…There was a close call once."

"Was I there?"

"Yes. You, me, and Dad were taking a trip to California."

"What happened?"

"Engine failure. Your dad managed to land the plane safely. It was a rough landing, but we all walked away unharmed."

"Who's all?"

"You, me, and Dad."

"Was there anyone else there? Like a woman? A family friend, maybe?"

"No. Why do you ask?"

"You know how I have nightmares and see images of a plane crash?"

"Yes."

"Well, there's more."

"You mean the mysterious lady?"

"Yes. How did you know? I don't remember telling you about her."

"Not long after your dad died, you started talking about a beautiful woman you kept dreaming about. You said she was an angel, and you were going to marry her. You were about six at the time."

"Then what happened?"

"Between the nightmares and the woman, I started to freak out. I was really worried about you. You were so young. So I took you to a psychologist."

"What did he say?"

"He said you were traumatized by your father's death."

"Duh. Did he tell you the reason for the dreams? And the visions of the woman?"

"Yes, he did, as a matter of fact."

Excitement coursed through Chase as he thought

about finally understanding why these things kept happening to him. "What was the reason?"

"He told me you were having trouble dealing with your grief, so you concocted an imaginary friend to help you through. You know, someone beautiful and kind, who made you feel loved and safe."

"Really? Sounds pretty lame to me." Chase tapped his shoe against the hardwood maple floor.

"Yes. He said the dreams and visions would go away once you resolved your feelings about your father's death."

"But nothing went away, Mom. The fiery crash scenes, the woman. They're still with me."

Mom wrinkled her forehead. She gave the sauce another stir and took some breadsticks out of the oven. She wiped her hands and sat down at the table. "*None* of it went away? Not even the dreams of the woman?"

"Nope."

"I'm so sorry, Chase. I thought you were over those fantasies."

"It's okay, Mom. I'm all right. But I need to get to the bottom of this."

Mom nodded silently and rose from her seat. She drained the hot noodles, placed them in a large bowl, and set the table.

"Do you want to see the psychologist again, honey?"

"Maybe. I'm going to try another route first."

"Let me know if there's anything else I can do to help, sweetie."

Chase scooped a big helping of pasta and put it on

his plate. He took a bite and swallowed. "There is this one thing you might be able to help with. Do we know anyone named Darla?"

"Your dad had a teacher named Darla when he was about seven years old. She was his favorite. Even helped him overcome his fear of reading aloud in class. He says because of her, he was able to speak at pilot conferences as an adult."

"Cool. Did I ever see Darla's picture?"

"No, sweetie. Why would you? What is this all about?"

"I'm curious," Chase lied. "Do you know what happened to her?"

"I'm not sure. Your dad only mentioned her a few times."

"Was Dad ever involved with her?"

"What do you mean by involved?"

"Like in a relationship. When he got older."

Mom gasped. "Oh, heavens no! She was eighteen years older than him. Why all these questions? What is going on?"

"I think Darla may be the woman in my dreams."

"Really? Why?"

"During my last vision, the mysterious woman sat next to me on the plane as it went down. Kaitlyn said I screamed and called out a name—Darla."

"Don't be silly, Chase! That doesn't mean anything."

"I think it does. I believe the woman in my dreams is named Darla. And since Dad knew a Darla, it must be her."

"But why would your dad's teacher be in your dreams and visions?"

"I don't know yet, but I plan to find out."

"How? What are you going to do?

"Well, I have an appointment with a hypnotherapist tomorrow. Maybe hypnosis will uncover a memory to help explain everything. I want to find Darla, too."

"Oh, Chase. I don't think hypnosis is such a good idea. It's so unconventional. Being put under might mess with your head. And I'm not sure finding your father's teacher will do any good, either. You don't want to intrude on some poor old woman's life. She may not even remember your father anymore. I think it's best to leave the past in the past."

"Sorry. I can't, Mom. I think there's a connection I'm missing. Maybe if I find Darla she can help clear things up."

Mom looked at him with the stern, scolding face he remembered so well from his childhood. "Please, Chase. Don't do something you'll regret. Leave your father's teacher out of this. Register for college courses, enjoy your life. Go see a reputable doctor, not some New Age quack. You have a bright future ahead of you. I don't want to see you disappointed or hurt."

"I'll be fine, Mom. I promise." Chase sprinkled Parmesan cheese on his pasta. "So, what's Darla's last name?"

"Chambers. Mrs. Darla Chambers."

"She was married?"

"I believe so."

"How old would she be today?"

"Hmm…Let me think…I'm not sure…she would probably be about…seventy."

"Thanks, Mom! I'll let you know what I find."

"Chase. Please, listen to me. This isn't a good idea."

"Trust me, Mom. I need to do this."

"You sound so determined. You're not running off right now, are you?"

"Nope. I have to finish this delicious spaghetti with my mom first. Then I'm off to the library to do some research."

☯☯☯

For his research to find Darla Chambers, Chase decided to visit the Macomb County Community College Library at Center campus. The library was close by, only fifteen minutes from his hometown of Sterling Heights, Michigan, in nearby Clinton Township. There was bound to be some information about his mystery woman there.

The library was quiet and not very busy. He figured everyone had better things to do on a Saturday night than hang out amid books and computers. Chase plopped himself down at a computer and got to work.

As he typed in Darla's name, a chill came over him. He didn't know if it was from excitement or the fear of the unknown, but he would soon have answers. This was an important step in his journey, a way to find out more about his visions and, ultimately, himself. He hoped he could pay Darla a visit and get to the bottom of why he was so connected to her and why she had been appearing to him all these years.

He scrolled through the search results on Darla, which both thrilled and terrified him. The first fact he found: Darla Chambers had a husband named Robert. For some odd reason, the name Robert Chambers rang a bell. Maybe it was just a common name. Anyway, those details weren't important. He needed to know more about Darla Chambers, not her husband.

As he scanned the search results, he also found an article in *The Macomb Daily* about how Darla had received a Teacher of the Year Award in 1971 at age 26. The story said Mrs. Chambers went above and beyond the call of duty and often spent her free time mentoring students. She also developed a new program called "Everyone's a Winner" to help build students' self-esteem and encourage them to embrace their unique talents and live up to their full potential.

Chase's heart thumped when he thought of what an incredible woman she was. He couldn't wait to meet her in person, even if she was an old lady now. They may not be able to have a relationship, but they could be friends or perhaps meet for coffee sometime. Chase smiled. To finally come face to face with his idol would truly be a dream come true.

His heart stopped, however, when he spotted the next item in his search results. Darla's obituary.

Mrs. Darla Chambers, age 28. Died July 11, 1973. Beloved wife of Robert and dear mother of Kendra. Mrs. Chambers was a caring and devoted teacher who worked tirelessly to bring greater levels of success and achievement to all her students.

Staring back at him was a picture of Darla, identical to how she had appeared in his dreams. Her brown hair was long and wavy, and her deep brown eyes exuded warmth and compassion. She was absolutely gorgeous.

Chase felt an unfathomable and profound sense of loss. Emotion overcame him, and he fought back tears. Not only was his mystery woman real now, but she had sadly died long ago. He would never be able to see her in person. He would never be able to give her a hug. The love he'd felt all these years was for a woman he could never meet.

Through blurry eyes, he struggled to read the rest of the obituary. It highlighted more details about Mrs. Chambers's exemplary work as a teacher and local church member. It talked about her caring personality and kindness to everyone, including strangers. And it mentioned her love and devotion to Robert and her toddler daughter Kendra.

Reading about her stirred up his own feelings surrounding the loss of his father as a small boy. It had been so hard growing up without a dad. Missed baseball and football games, school concerts, and family vacations. No father-son fishing trips or visits to the ballpark. He had missed out on it all. Kendra hadn't even gotten to really know her mom and most likely didn't remember her. At least he had some memories of his father.

What happened to Darla? Chase wondered. *Why did she die so young?*

He searched for her name and the word "died." What he found next was even more unexpected. Darla Chambers had lost her life in a plane crash, along with her husband. Apparently, they were on their way to Hawaii for their fifth anniversary when the plane got caught in a severe thunderstorm and experienced engine trouble. The plane had caught fire and exploded into pieces when it hit the ground. The pilot, as well as all 223 passengers and crew members, died.

The scene Chase knew so well flashed through his mind again. He had been seeing visions of Darla's plane crash! It wasn't about him at all. He hadn't been on board the plane, but somehow, he had been experiencing the fear and turmoil as if he were actually there.

But why the romantic dreams? If she wasn't a part of his future and they were never to meet, then why did he dream of them together? Why did he feel like he was in love with her? None of this made any sense.

He couldn't wait to tell the therapist everything tomorrow. In the meantime, he felt compelled to tell someone. It had to be Kaitlyn. She was the only one who would understand and not ridicule him for believing in the paranormal.

He pulled his phone from his pocket and shot her a text. *Kate, please call me.*

Within minutes, his phone buzzed. He sprang from his seat and moved to the lobby to talk. "Kate?"

"Chase? Are you okay?"

"Yeah. I'm all right."

"What's going on? You scared me."

"Sorry. I really need to talk to you right now. Can

you meet me?”

“Sure. Where are you?”

“I’m at the library now. How ’bout we meet at Dodge Park? By the walking paths?”

“Okay. I’m on my way.”

☯☯☯

Chase was struck by Kaitlyn’s beauty when he saw her standing by the trails at Dodge Park. She always put forth a lot of time and effort to look flawless. This time was different. She looked more natural, without all the makeup and dressy clothes. She was even more gorgeous in plain jeans and a purple T-shirt. The sun sat low in the sky, and its rays glistened in her golden hair. Her eyes lit up when she saw him, and they ran to each other for a hug. Chase felt a twinge of sadness for the girlfriend he had given up. They could have been a great couple if only he was more into her.

“Missed me already?” she teased.

“Always.” He laughed.

Her expression turned serious, and she grabbed his hand and pulled him toward the path. “So what do you want to tell me?”

“I found some information about my so-called dream girl at the library.”

“Oh, Chase, that’s great! So she’s real then?”

“Yes. One problem though. She’s already dead.”

“What? How sad.”

“Yeah. I talked to my mom to see if she could help explain my visions. She said my dad’s favorite teacher was named Darla. She really helped him a lot, and he never forgot her. So, I went to the library to search for her. Thought maybe I could get some answers. Turns out Darla died in a plane crash with her husband in 1973. When I saw her obituary, the picture looked exactly like my dream woman. It was so freaky. Turns out I've been seeing visions of her death."

"Incredible! So do you think you were being visited by Darla's ghost instead of seeing the future?"

"Yeah. I think so. Only I have no idea why."

"Guardian angel?"

"Could be. But I never knew her, so why would she watch over me?"

"I read some people have spirit guides they've never met in real life."

"True. But why the romantic stuff then?"

"I really couldn't tell you. Are you going to see another psychic medium?"

"Actually, I'm reading a book I got from the psychic in Panama City. It's about a hypnotherapy technique called regression therapy. I also made an appointment with a hypnotherapist for tomorrow."

"Awesome, Chase. I hope you get to the bottom of things soon."

"Me too...There's one other thing I need to ask you."

"Okay. Shoot."

"Darla had a daughter. Her name was Kendra. She'd be in her mid-40s today. I know your uncle is a private investigator. Could you give me his number?"

"Of course," she said with a nod.

"I thought maybe if I found Kendra, she could tell me more about Darla so I can understand why I've been dreaming about her and seeing visions of her plane crash."

"Sounds like a good plan. I'll text you his number right now."

"Great. Thank you."

Kaitlyn pulled out her phone and sent him the number. Then she grabbed his hand.

"Come with me," she urged. "I need to talk to you, too."

Chase followed her as she guided him deeper into the woods until they were out of sight.

"I think what I have to say will help you," she whispered.

"Okay."

"All of my life, I've pretended to be someone I'm not. I wanted so desperately to be liked, to be popular. I wanted the boys to adore me."

"Well, it worked."

"I'm not done yet." She nudged him. "Everyone thinks I'm this confident girl who's got it all. But on the inside, I'm scared and insecure, like you. Believe it or not, I had a very difficult past."

"Really? What do you mean?"

Kaitlyn took a deep breath and paused for a few minutes. She ran her hand through her hair and nervously picked at her fingernails. Her eyes filled with tears, and she breathed erratically. When she finally spoke, Chase almost didn't recognize her voice. It was very soft and shaky, not at all like the flamboyant, self-assured girl he usually saw.

"You have to promise to never breathe a word of this to anyone."

"I promise," he said, joining his pinky with hers. "Your secret's safe with me."

"When I was seven years old—at my old school—I wasn't very popular. My parents didn't have much money then, so I wore hand-me-downs from my cousins."

"Nooo! Call the press. Kaitlyn wore used clothing."

She grabbed his arm and stopped him. "I'm being totally serious here. This is a big deal to me."

"Sorry. I'm listening."

"Anyway. The kids used to tease me and call me 'trash can girl.' They said my clothes weren't cool like theirs, and I belonged in a dumpster."

"Oh, Kate."

"I used to cry every day. I wanted so badly to fit in, but no one would play with me. There was this one girl, Sabrina, who was the meanest of all. Every day on the way home from school, she would threaten to beat me up. I was terrified." A tear rolled down Kaitlyn's cheek.

Chase gave her a reassuring hug and stroked her hair. "It's okay. You can tell me anything."

"I know. You don't judge me. Not many guys are like you, Chase."

"You're a great girl. It's not hard to like you."

"Thanks." She smiled slightly, and then continued her story. "One night I had a strange dream. A lady came to me and told me not to be afraid; everything would be okay. She said my family would be moving soon, but first I would go through something awful. She showed me a vision of myself lying on the ground bleeding from the mouth. I was horrified."

"What a nightmare!"

"Only it wasn't a nightmare. A couple of weeks later, when I left school a bit late, Sabrina was out back waiting for me. She pushed me to the ground and punched me hard. I got a bloody nose and lost a tooth. Like in my vision, I bled from the mouth. I sobbed and begged her to stop. She called me a baby."

"I'm so sorry that happened to you, Kaitlyn."

She nodded. "Sabrina was so much bigger than me. She managed to lift me up and toss me right into the dumpster. Then she said I was right where I belonged, in the trash. I was so humiliated!"

"Did you tell anyone?"

"No. I was too scared and embarrassed. Then the following week, my dad got a job offer in Detroit. We packed up and moved here. And I met you."

"Wow, Kate. I didn't realize you went through so much."

"I was different back then. I never stood up to anyone. I felt like a worthless person. I was weak, lonely, and embarrassed. So I understand how it feels to not fit in. I may not know exactly what you're going through right now. But I get it."

Chase held out his arms and wrapped them around her, squeezing tight. "I'm so sorry. I wish I could have been there for you."

"It's okay. I want you to know you don't have to go through your struggles alone. I'm still here if you need me, as a friend."

"Thanks."

"There's something else I need to tell you, too."

She leaned in closer. Chase kicked a stick on the ground below with his foot, uncertain of what she was about to say.

"I know why our relationship as a couple doesn't work," she said.

"You do?"

"Yes. I went to another psychic when we got back home. She says you and I were brother and sister in a past life. You always looked out for me back then, like you do now."

Chase laughed. "Did you believe her?"

"I don't know." She squinted and then smiled thoughtfully. "But it sure would make sense. She even claimed I was bullied in a previous life, and you were the one who came to my aid."

Chase nodded. He had never believed anyone could live more than once. And if it were possible, why would they? This life brought more than its share of suffering.

Kaitlyn looked down at the ground and kicked a rock. "One more thing," she said.

"What's up?"

She walked over to the park bench and sat down. She folded her hands in her lap and stared at the ground. Chase followed her.

"I know we were supposed to go to prom together. But someone else asked me after we broke up. I told him I would go with him. I hope you're not mad."

"Of course not. We're not a couple anymore. You

should be dating other guys. Besides, how are you going to find the relationship the psychic talked about if you don't go out with anyone?"

"Good point. But I hope you know, you'll always be my first true love. I wish things could have been different."

"Yeah, I know. It wasn't in the cards for us, sis," he teased, giving her a nudge.

She smiled warmly.

Chase held out his hand and helped her off of the bench. The birds chirped in the trees above, and the warm spring air smelled like lilies of the valley, which bloomed in a nearby perennial garden. "C'mon," he said. "It's a nice evening. Let's take a walk."

They trekked down a trail that meandered through the trees. Purple crocuses and white hydrangeas had begun their spring bloom along the path, and Chase and Kaitlyn stopped for a moment to admire them. As they traveled deeper into the woods, the evening sun filtered through the leaves above them and created magical shimmers. Chase couldn't help but wish Darla was alive, young, and his real-life girlfriend. He could almost see the two of them holding hands and kissing amid the privacy of the trees. He hoped to find a love like that one day.

Kaitlyn stopped along the path and picked a tiny wildflower. She placed it behind her ear and drew in a deep breath. The sunlight in her hair made her look like some sort of golden goddess. She was stunning. If only things were different, he would kiss her right now. But his heart belonged elsewhere.

Sensing his distress, Kaitlyn walked over to him and wrapped her arms around him. She planted a soft kiss on his cheek and whispered in his ear, “I’m glad we’re still friends.”

They held each other for a few minutes, and Chase got the feeling they were saying good-bye. Not to each other or to the friendship they had always shared. Instead, they were finally putting their romantic relationship behind them. It was time for them both to move on. Chase felt a little sad, but sorrow was overpowered by an intense feeling of freedom and hope for the future.

Chase didn’t know how long they stood there, holding each other close one last time, but a crackling in the woods startled both of them.

Kaitlyn whispered again in Chase’s ear. “I think we’re being watched.”

He felt it, too. Someone or something was spying on them. Chase wasn’t about to stick around to see what lurked beyond the trees. He still felt very protective of Kaitlyn and knew he had to do whatever he could to keep her out of danger. “C’mon,” he said quietly. “Let’s go the other way. Another trail winds around the back of the park.”

“Chase. I’m creeped out.”

“It’s okay,” he said, putting an arm around her. “You’re safe with me. I won’t let anything happen to you.”

Cracking branches signaled the person or animal was on the move. Chase grabbed Kaitlyn’s hand, and they began running. Panting, and with hearts pounding, they hurried all the way through the alternate trail. Neither of them dared look back.

CHAPTER 9
THE ONE THAT GOT AWAY

Willow threw herself down on the plush red sofa and sobbed. Her dreams had once again been shattered, like the night of the terrible accident all those years ago. She had followed him again tonight and spotted him in the arms of another woman. At least she thought it was him. She had been closer this time, hidden barely out of sight. He looked younger than she thought he would be, but those eyes—she would recognize them anywhere. Deep brown and compassionate. It had to be Rob.

Sadly, he was with the same pretty blonde from a couple of weeks ago. She could tell the other woman meant something to him, and her heart ached deeply. She gasped for air as those painful, yet familiar, feelings of despair and separation flooded her mind. She had lost him once again. How would she go on? She couldn't bear the thought of living without him. Especially not when she had finally found him and was so close to reuniting with him.

Willow buried her face in the white throw pillow and cried some more. Then she hugged the pillow tight and sat up. This was not how their story was supposed to end.

She thought of the last time they had seen each other. He'd been beside her, so handsome and strong, his eyes welling up with tears as they said their good-byes. Their situation was tragic, but their love remained unbreakable, and they'd pledged to find each other again someday. She knew they would move heaven and Earth to be together. She couldn't give up now. Not when she had gotten this close. She had to fight for him.

Yes, she would continue to watch and wait for the right moment. She would look for signs he missed her, too, and longed for the breathtaking, soul-stirring love they had once shared, the love they would always share. She knew him better than anyone, and the Rob she knew and loved was loyal, committed, and devoted to her. Surely, he felt the emptiness inside, too. In his heart, he must know she was out there, waiting for him. Somehow, somewhere, someday…their love would find a way.

☯☯☯

After he and Kaitlyn had safely escaped the intruder in the park, Chase called the private investigator. A sense of urgency now propelled him forward, and he was thirsty for as many facts as he could gather. His research into Darla's past had ignited the sleuth in him, and he was determined to make sense of his life and his many unexplained experiences.

An older man with a raspy voice answered. "Jerry Green, private investigator."

"Oh, hello, Mr. Green," Chase said, trying to sound professional and not too excited. "I'm Chase, your niece Kaitlyn's friend."

"Hello, Chase. What I can do for you?"

"I need to find someone. Do you think you can help?"

"Of course. And I'll tell you what...since you know Kaitlyn, I'll give you a discount rate, $20 per hour. Sound good?"

"Yes. I really appreciate that, Mr. Green."

"No problem. So, what do you need?"

"Well, there's this woman who was my dad's teacher many years ago. Her name is Darla Chambers. She died, but I would like to find her daughter Kendra."

"Okay. Let me explain a little about I usually operate. First, I jot down as much information as you can give me—names, cities, schools, relatives. Then I search all of the relevant databases and collect as much data as I can. Next, I make calls and visit the locations where the person may be. I check both public records as well as police reports, hospital records, and legal documents. Finally, I put together a detailed file, which typically includes the person's full name, address, phone number, marital status, and place of employment as well as any tickets, convictions, or arrests. Once my investigation is complete, I supply all the information to you."

"Sounds great. When can we get started?"

"Well, if you have a few minutes, we can talk now."

"Of course, sir."

"Okay then. So tell me, what do you know about Kendra?"

"Not much," Chase confessed. "I know she was a toddler when her mom died in 1973. Her dad was Robert Chambers. They lived in the area."

"Those meager details aren't a lot to go on, son. Do you know more?"

"I know where Mrs. Chambers is buried and where she taught school. I also know Kendra would be in her mid-forties now. The last known address was here in Michigan."

"Every little bit of information helps. Do you know if Kendra was married?"

"No, I'm afraid I don't."

"Okay. Email me the details you have, and I'll see what I can do. I should be able to give you a call with some leads in a week or two."

"No problem, Mr. Green." He jotted down the email address the investigator rattled off. "Thanks for doing this."

"You're welcome, son. I hope you find what you're looking for."

"Me too."

Chase hung up and quickly sent an email from his phone. When he'd sent it, he started his car and pulled out of the parking lot, ready to go home for the night. His head now throbbed, and he was in desperate need of some rest. He had only been home from the airport for less than four hours, and so much had already happened. He knew the identity of his dream woman and had enlisted a private investigator's help to find her daughter. And, he no longer had a date for his senior prom, which was only a few days away. The tornado had picked up momentum and was about to whisk him off to who knew where. He only hoped Justine, the therapist, would be able to help.

☯☯☯

Justine was slightly older than Chase's mom, with graying blonde hair and kind green eyes. She was soft spoken and wore gold, wire-rimmed glasses. Whenever Chase spoke, her eyebrows would rise above the rims as if she were either surprised or skeptical.

"How very odd," Justine said as Chase explained his story about Darla, the plane crash visions, and the dreams. "I've never had a client who dreamed of a dead woman in such a way."

She scribbled some notes on a piece of paper and took a sip of coffee from her cat-shaped mug.

"How do people usually dream of the dead?" Chase asked.

"Well, sometimes they have nightmares about how the person died, but in those cases they usually know them. You didn't know this woman, so dreaming about her death is rather unusual."

"And what else?"

"Other times, the dreams are more like visits.

Clients report they feel very real and vivid, like they are actually with the person who died. Some people really believe their deceased loved one has come to comfort them, provide guidance, or say good-bye."

"What do you believe?"

"I believe in a higher power. I'm not sure if the dead can actually visit us, but I like to keep an open mind. Anything's possible, I guess."

"So then Darla could be my guardian angel. Maybe she's watching over me like she did with the kids she taught. My dad could have asked her in heaven to keep an eye on me."

"Interesting theory. But why the romantic relationship then?"

"I don't know."

"Does it bother you to have dreams and visions of this kind?"

"No. I like them." He grinned, thinking of how invigorating Darla's soft skin and lips felt against his. "I'm bummed they can never happen in real life."

"I suppose that would be rather disappointing." She crossed her legs and took another sip of her coffee.

"Yeah, it's a real drag. I thought my dreams were glimpses of the future. I believed Darla was someone I would meet and hook up with. Now I know it'll never happen."

"Do you have a girlfriend now?"

"I did. We broke up."

"Are you sad?"

"A little. Kaitlyn's a great girl and all. She's even my best friend. But she isn't…"

"Her?"

"Yeah, she isn't Darla. I don't feel the same way about her."

"But your dream girl is—a dream. You can never have her. Kaitlyn is in the real world. Why would you trade a great girlfriend for someone you can never have? Are you afraid of commitment? Are you afraid of love?"

"Don't think so."

"Then what?"

Chase cleared his throat. "When I first called things off with Kaitlyn, I believed Darla and I would be together one day. I didn't know she was my father's teacher and that even if she were alive, she would be seventy years old. I certainly couldn't have a relationship with a lady old enough to be my grandmother."

Justine raised her eyebrows again, and a little squeak came out of her mouth. She pushed her glasses up and scratched her nose as if she were contemplating something. "So now that you know Darla is not really your ideal girlfriend, do you want Kaitlyn back?"

"Sometimes. But I still feel like the right girl is out there and I haven't met her yet."

"A lot of people share your sentiments. But remember, you can't wait your whole life for the perfect person. Sometimes the image we create in our heads of the ideal partner is a fairy tale."

"Mine wasn't a fairy tale. Darla *was* a real person. If she existed, then maybe there's someone out there like her. Someone I need to find."

"Only you know what's best for you," Justine said. "However, I want to be sure you don't have an idealized image of what love is supposed to be like. Otherwise, you'll be waiting forever."

"I know. It scares me to think I could wind up alone. I mean, I'm not ready to get married or anything, but I think I would like to someday."

"So tell me more about your other dreams and visions…about the plane crash," she encouraged.

"Actually, it feels more like a flashback. It's as if I'm sitting right there on the plane when the pilot makes the announcement. I can see and feel everything. It sucks!"

"Nightmares often feel like real life."

"True. But the crash I see and dream of, it actually happened."

"Whatever do you mean, dear?"

"When I searched for Darla, I found out she died in a plane crash."

Justine gasped. "Oh, heavens." Her eyebrows rose higher than Chase had seen them so far.

"The details of the crash from the newspaper article actually matched my vision. It's like I knew what happened without ever knowing I did."

"How very bizarre. Your case is unlike any other I've encountered. I think you need more than straight hypnosis. Possibly regression therapy would help."

Chase perked up. He thought of the psychic in Panama City and what she'd told him. He also remembered what he'd read in her book: many tough cases were successfully resolved when a therapist dug into a client's past with regression therapy and addressed repressed memories and trauma. "Yes, I've read a little about it. Do you do regression therapy?"

"Unfortunately, no. I'm not equipped to help you figure this one out. It goes way behind my scope of knowledge."

"You mean you're bailing on me already?"

"No, Chase, but I would like you to see Dr. Whitgard. He's a hypnotherapist who's handled some extraordinary cases. He specializes in regression therapy and might be able to help you."

"Okay, if you think so."

She reached into her desk drawer, pulled out a business card, and extended her hand. "Here's his card. Please give him a call."

"I will. Thanks."

☯☯☯

Whenever Chase needed time to think, he retreated into a quiet world of his own, which often lead him to his favorite safe haven, Lincoln Park. His session with Justine had disappointed him. He'd expected so much more than a few raised eyebrows and a referral to see someone else. Was there anyone who could help him? Should he even bother to call Dr. Whitgard?

Chase pulled into the park and sighed. He hoped the tranquil setting would help lead him to the right choices and the right answers. Life and the world had steered him wrong, for sure. Now, weeks away from his high school graduation, he still struggled to find himself. Confusion and emptiness were his constant companions, and he had little idea what made him tick. Who was

Chase? What were the secrets locked deep inside him? He needed to know now, more than ever.

He got out of the car and walked across the parking lot. He searched for something—anything—to bring some clarity to his muddled thoughts.

The playground area of the park overflowed with spunky kids who ran and climbed the monkey bars. Motivated walkers and bikers in cotton shorts and tank tops breezed along the paths. The world closed in on him, and he needed to escape its constant buzz. He walked further, determined to find a peaceful, secluded spot.

As he trekked deeper into the trails, a quiet solitude seeped in. The trees alongside him, and their thick branches and leaves above, formed a shield from the outside world. Soon, all he noticed were nature's refreshing little nuances. Tiny animals chattered as they scurried about, and the wind whistled as it blew through the trees. The air brushed across his skin like a gentle caress, bringing further awareness. He smelled the rich scents of pine, maple, and fir with a faint touch of wildflowers. He was at home here.

At the end of the longest trail sat a lone wooden park bench. It was nestled in a quiet spot among the trees near a small pond. Often when he was there, his fears melted away, and he became more grounded. He could temporarily forget his life wasn't the way he wanted it to be. Sometimes, he would simply sit and breathe in the fresh air. Other times, he would skip rocks along the surface of the pond or feed the ducks. He was almost always alone there, since few visitors traveled so deep into the park.

Until now.

A figure of a girl emerged from the woods as Chase sat on his favorite park bench. Her brown hair was lit with gold in the sunlight, and she appeared to be in her mid-twenties. He couldn't get a clear view of her, but she was alone and studying him intently. A thrill coursed through his body. Had she been the one spying on Kaitlyn and him in the woods last night?

He squinted in the sunlight and looked between the trees where she quietly stood. He couldn't make out her face, so he rose from his seat and began to approach her. She darted into the woods and quickly disappeared.

Even though she had run away, she had awakened something inside him. He wondered who she was and why she kept spying on him. Was he supposed to meet her for some reason? What did she want? And why was she so afraid to talk to him? He had to know.

Chase now knew what he needed to do next. He would call Dr. Whitgard and make an appointment. He would wait to hear from Jerry Green with news on Darla's daughter Kendra. And he would make a point of coming here each day to the same spot to look for the girl in the woods.

His life was shrouded in mystery. It was time to lift the veil and see what lurked beneath.

CHAPTER 10
FLASH FROM THE PAST

A quiet emptiness filled Dr. Whitgard's office, which caught Chase off guard. Apparently, the doctor worked alone. Maybe he found it easier to perform hypnosis with fewer distractions. Chase kind of liked the silence anyway. It reminded him of his secluded retreat at the park.

Chase sat in the waiting room and scanned the surroundings. A blue and green checkered area rug sat in front of a tan leather sofa. Across from him, he noticed two tan leather chairs with wooden peg legs and blue and green pillows. On the wall above hung a simple framed painting of a sandy beach. The blue water perfectly coordinated with the colors of the rug and accent pillows. The whole room exuded tastefulness, simplicity, and peace. Chase sighed and slowed his thoughts. He had a good feeling about this.

The door opened, and a man popped out. Dr.

Whitgard looked like a cross between a mad scientist and Jesus. His long, unkempt brown-gray hair hung down in greasy waves, and his ribs protruded slightly through his thin white shirt. His exuberant face was partly hidden behind a long, thick, bushy beard. But his brilliant blue eyes were what stood out the most. They resembled the sky on a cloudless day. Piercing, yet mesmerizing. Inviting, yet mysterious.

Chase watched as he shuffled through the lobby doorway and eagerly extended his hand.

"Hello. Hello. Welcome," he said. "I am Dr. Henry Whitgard. It's such a pleasure to make your acquaintance."

He spoke at lightning speed, and Chase wondered if the doctor was in a hurry or simply enthused. Either way, he was ready to do this.

"Chase," he said as he shook the doctor's hand.

"Did your parents chase you around the house a lot? Or do you enjoy the thrill of the chase?" He flashed a silly, toothy grin and motioned for him to follow.

"Umm. Nooo."

Dr. Whitgard let out a big, hearty laugh in stark contrast to his scrawny, frail body. "I'm joking with you." He opened his office door and led Chase inside.

His office décor included lots of brown furniture—a leather couch, two leather chairs, and an oversized walnut desk with a small globe trimmed in gold. Chase chose the couch, and Dr. Whitgard sat down in the large armchair directly across from him.

Chase gave him a weak smile and looked away. "Aha!" Dr. Whitgard said as if making an important discovery. "It's all clear to me now. You're one of those types."

Chase sat up straighter in his chair and looked at the doctor, feeling puzzled. "What type?" He shifted in his seat as blood rushed to his cheeks. How dare the doctor presume things about him when he didn't even know him?

"Hold it in. Lock it away. Run and hide. Some of my clients would have told me off. You tuned me out when I poked fun at you."

"I didn't want to be impolite, sir."

"It's not about politeness. It's about expressing yourself. It's about *feelings.* What are you feeling, Chase? Do you even know? What happened to you, and why is it affecting you still? This is what we need to uncover. These questions will unlock the secrets of the real Chase, your true self."

"Okay. Fine," Chase said, raising his voice. "I can't believe you would make fun of my name. I mean, what kind of a therapist are you?"

"A darn good one, actually." Dr. Whitgard smoothed his rumpled, white, button-down shirt with his hand and leaned forward.

"Well, then, prove it to me."

"All right then. First things first. Why are you here?"

Chase explained the visions and nightmares of the plane crash, followed by details about Darla. He told Dr. Whitgard about his strong feelings for her and how he had discovered she was a real person who had died. By the end of his story, Chase had tears in his eyes.

"Very good! Now we're getting somewhere!" Dr. Whitgard exclaimed. He rose from his seat and went over to a whiteboard hanging on the adjacent wall. He grabbed a marker and wrote *Darla, died in plane crash.* Then he looked at Chase. "So, this Darla. She's very important to you?"

"Yes."

"And you want to be with her again?"

"Well, sort of. Only I was never really *with* her."

"I'm sorry," he corrected. "I mean, you want to be with her in your dreams again?"

"Of course."

"These dreams…would you say they feel more real than real life?"

"Yes, I would."

"Interesting." He placed his hand under his bearded chin. "And what else, Chase? Tell me more."

"I want to understand why I dream of her and why I knew how she died."

He again turned to the white board and wrote: *Encounters feel real. Why? How?* "Very good. Lots of whys. It's always important to ask questions."

"But I want the answers. I *need* the answers."

"Yes, yes. And that's why we're here."

"So can you help me, Doc?"

"I do believe I can."

"How?"

Dr. Whitgard quickly scribbled something on the whiteboard and underlined it twice, then he turned to face Chase. He pointed to the words *regression therapy.* "I believe *this* is the answer," he said confidently.

"Ah, yes. I read a bit about it last week. Both a psychic and another hypnotherapist recommended it."

"Well, they're on the right track. Regression therapy is a simple, yet powerful, type of hypnosis. Essentially, it helps us to focus on resolving significant past life events that may be interfering with your current emotional state and wreaking havoc on your well-being."

"Sounds good to me."

Dr. Whitgard sat down on the leather chair again and ran his finger through his messy beard. "I'm going to take you back in time and space to a place you may not remember. As you recall memories from this distant place, you will gain a better understanding of yourself and what has brought you to where you are today."

"Okay."

"Are you ready then, Chase? Are you ready to travel back in time in your mind?"

"Yep."

"Very well. Let's get started."

Dr. Whitgard grabbed his notepad and pen and cleared his throat. "First, take a slow deep breath. Inhale through your nose and exhale through your mouth. Breathe in peace and knowing; breathe out stress, conflict, worry, and the unknown. Release all negative emotions from your body. Let go."

Chase did as the doctor instructed and began to relax. His shoulders were no longer crammed up into his ears, and his stomach unknotted. His mind drifted.

"Good."

Dr. Whitgard switched on some New Age music,

which reminded Chase of a trip to a spa. A flute played softly, accompanied by the soothing sounds of ocean waves hitting the shore. Chase could actually picture himself there, walking along the beach, hand in hand with Darla.

"Now, I want you to count with me. One. You are feeling more relaxed and freer than you have in a long time. Two. You are ready for the truth. It is ready to reveal itself to you. Three. So very relaxed. You're a wispy cloud floating through the sky. You are free to embrace all you are and all you were in the past. I want you to travel back in time now to your childhood. Where are you now?"

Chase saw himself as a young boy. He and his mom stood holding hands at his father's gravesite, under a large oak tree on a grassy hill. They both cried. Mom handed him a tissue and tossed a red rose on the grave. She turned to leave.

Chase grabbed her hand and urged her to stay. "Wait, Mommy. There's something we didn't do yet."

"What is it?" she asked.

"We didn't tell Daddy we love him."

"Bill," she began. "I love you more than the stars and the moon. I miss you every day and will continue to miss you the rest of my life. Thank you for blessing us with our handsome son, Chase, and for being a model father and husband. Our lives aren't the same without you. I wish you were here with us so much."

She began to sob. Her cries echoed through the cemetery like the screechy calls of birds. It was a painful moment for them both.

"I miss him too, Mommy," Chase said. He looked down at his father's gravestone, then up to the sky. "Daddy, I love you very much. Please send an angel from heaven to watch over me and Mommy. Thank you!"

A gentle breeze drifted across Chase's cheek, and he felt as if he were being kissed. His young self was certain his father had heard him and would honor his request.

He described the scene to the doctor.

"Good. Good," Dr. Whitgard said. "You're reliving a past memory. Now I want you to do something else."

"Okay."

"I would like you to envision a scene with the woman Darla. Imagine you are with her right now. What are you doing? How do you feel?"

Chase closed his eyes and concentrated. Within a few minutes, he saw Darla standing in front of him on a beautiful beach. The waves gently rolled against the shore while the sun cast glittering shadows upon them. A bright blue sky provided the perfect backdrop for a day together. Darla slipped off her shoes, and Chase did the same. They held hands and walked along the water's edge. Seagulls squawked overhead and seemed to be cheering them on. He felt happy by Darla's side.

"I see Darla and me on the beach. I feel happy."

"Very good," he said enthusiastically. "Now I want you to talk to her."

"Talk to her? But I would be making this all up."

"It's okay. Don't worry about the details. Ask her a question. What do you want to know?"

"Darla, why are you here with me?"

She tossed her gorgeous long brown hair back and laughed. "Easy, silly, because I love you."

"But how can you love me? We've never even met."

"Of course we have!" she objected. "You're here with me now, aren't you?"

"But you're not real. You're a figment of my imagination."

"Do you really think I exist only in your imagination?"

"What else could it be?"

"Dig a little deeper," she suggested.

"Are you my guardian angel?"

"Could be," she said with a grin. "You'll find the answers when the time is right." She stopped walking and softly kissed Chase's lips before fading from view.

"She's gone now," Chase said sadly.

"What did she tell you?"

"She said she's with me because she loves me."

"And do you believe her, Chase?"

"I want to. But how could she love me? We've never even met. She died before I was born. It doesn't make any sense."

"It doesn't make sense now, but I suspect it will one day," Dr. Whitgard said encouragingly. "Let's bring you out of hypnosis now, and we'll pick this back up next time."

Chase listened to Dr. Whitgard's soothing voice as he counted backward from ten to one. When the doctor finished, Chase was alert and felt as if he had woken up from a refreshing dream.

"Do you remember anything?"

"Yes, I remember being at the cemetery with my mom after Dad died. And I remember spending time on the beach with Darla."

"Excellent." He recorded some notes on his pad, and then typed something on his laptop before rising from his seat. "We'll continue this next time. I want to see you again on Thursday."

"I still feel so confused though. I don't understand why any of this is happening."

"No worries," Dr. Whitgard said reassuringly. "Give it time. It will all make sense one day."

Chase almost jumped out of his seat when his cell phone rang as he drove home from his session with Dr. Whitgard. The hands-free device on his console called out "*incoming call from Jerry Green.*" A wave of excitement rippled through him. Maybe now he could finally get somewhere. He pushed the car radio button to answer.

"Hello?"

"Hello, Chase. It's Jerry Green."

"Mr. Green, I'm so glad to hear from you."

Mr. Green sighed. "I'm afraid I have bad news, son."

"Did you find anything on Kendra?"

"As a matter of fact, I did. Unfortunately, Kendra died a couple of years ago. She was the victim of domestic violence. I can tell you where she's buried, but not much else."

A twinge of sadness ran through Chase. Another dead end? Why was this happening to him? Darla was gone and so was her daughter. How would he ever find the truth?

"That sucks."

"I know. I'm really sorry, son. If you need anything else, please give me a call. But I'm afraid this case is closed."

"Okay. Thanks."

"No problem. I hope you find what you're looking for someday."

"I hope so, too."

Chase hung up the phone and slammed his hands against the steering wheel. He was no closer to discovering the truth than when he'd first started. In fact, he was even further from it. To make matters worse, he felt even more alone than he had been in a long time. The empty space in his chest had grown, and a longing invaded his soul. His car followed the curve in the road, a desolate road with no cars and no signs of people. He drove ahead into the darkness, not sure what awaited.

Dr. Whitgard was clearly his last hope now. Maybe the doc could uncover something about Chase's past, and everything would finally fit into place. Chase knew one thing for sure: his past still haunted him, and it wouldn't let go. Now his dreams for the future had been short-circuited, too. Darla and Kendra were gone. Yet he still longed for something, someone. A persistent craving for a love and life he would never have filled his heart. A part of him was missing. Would he ever find it?

The shallowness surrounded him as he pulled into the driveway of his house. He remained trapped in a complex puzzle he couldn't fully comprehend.

All around him, the dark night settled in. The day had come to an end; it was time to give up for now.

Or was it? Chase suddenly had an urge to drive to Lincoln Park, his solace.

He backed out of the driveway and pointed the car in the direction of the park. Maybe he'd see her, the unknown girl who was watching him so intently yesterday. Something about her intrigued him. He had to know more.

When he arrived at the park a few minutes later, an unusual sense of calmness came over him. He headed to his favorite wooden park bench and sat down. The quiet stillness welcomed him like an old friend. The air had a slight chill to it but was somehow comforting, almost like all of his fears and confusion were being cleansed.

He breathed in deeply and went over the events of the past couple of weeks: his breakup with Kaitlyn, spring break, the psychic, the therapist, the mysterious girl in the park, finding out Darla and Kendra had died, his session with Dr. Whitgard. Everything he had experienced brought him to a single conclusion: he needed to talk to someone connected to Darla. He longed to know more about her, and why he felt this strange connection to her. Wasn't there anyone else who could shed light on her life?

Then it hit him like a ton of bricks and woke him out of a deep slumber. Maybe Kendra had a child!

Maybe Darla's grandchild was still alive and knew something to help clear his confusion.

He pulled his cell phone from his pocket and dialed Jerry Green.

"Hello. Jerry Green, P.I. here."

"Mr. Green, it's Chase."

"Chase? Is something up?"

"Maybe, sir. I had a thought."

"What is it?"

"When you searched for Darla's daughter, Kendra, did you find any other living relatives?"

"Actually, I did. But you didn't express an interest in finding anyone but Kendra, so I never mentioned it. Kendra has a daughter. Let me grab the file, and I can tell you more about her."

A renewed sense of hope came over Chase as he waited for Mr. Green to come back on the line. Maybe this girl could help. She might know some enlightening details about her grandmother. If nothing else, he could get to know his dream girl better through her granddaughter. Chase wanted so badly to feel connected to Darla in the physical world and not solely in his mind. He wanted to really *know* her.

As he thought about Darla and the possibility of meeting her grandchild, he heard a rustling in the woods across from him. He once again got the distinct feeling someone or something was watching him. He was about to get up from his seat and check it out when Mr. Green returned to the phone.

"Chase?"

"Yeah. I'm still here. Whatcha got?"

Chase stared at the spot in the woods where the noise had come from, but all was still and quiet now. However, he couldn't shake the feeling the person or animal was still there, carefully observing him.

"Daughter's name is Willow Haverly. She's twenty-three years old. I don't have a current address or phone number for her. It looks like she moved recently. But I can get more information for you in a couple of days."

"Okay. Great!"

"I'll be in touch, son."

"Thanks, Mr. Green."

Chase put his cell back in his sweatshirt pocket when the sound of a stick breaking directed his attention to the woods again. Someone was obviously still watching him from the dark shadows of the park. He peered into the darkness and studied the spot where the noise had come from. He was afraid to turn his head or look away.

Slowly, a figure emerged. Chase couldn't see her face, but her silhouette reminded him of Darla. Had she come to visit him from the afterlife? Did she know what he was going through?

"Who's there?" Chase called.

The woman didn't answer, but stood there watching him. He rose from his seat and began to approach her. She turned and ran.

"Wait. Wait," Chase cried. "I don't want to hurt you."

But how did she really know? He would run, too, if he were her. Seeing a man alone in the park after dark was rarely a safe situation. He chased after her, but she was faster than him. He lost sight of her again.

Chase wondered what a young woman was doing alone in the park after dark. Was she in trouble? Had she come to escape from something, or did she want some time alone to think like him? Could she be part of the bigger picture?

CHAPTER 11
UNEXPECTED ENCOUNTER

What a close call!

He'd almost caught her. Willow's heart pounded, and she felt sweaty and breathless. A part of her wanted him to catch her. She longed to be in his strong arms again. But the rest of her was plain scared. She had to get a closer look somehow, face-to-face, to be certain it was really Rob. She didn't want to embarrass herself by approaching the wrong person. And she couldn't stand the thought of him rejecting her if he'd moved on with someone else.

She looked down at her grandmother's ring. It sparkled in the moonlight as if to say everything would be all right.

"Please bring me luck. Please let Rob and me be together again. Let us share what you and Grandpa shared."

Even though her grandmother had died before

Willow was born, she had passed down some remarkable traits. Strength. Perseverance. Loyalty. Compassion. She'd had them all. She'd possessed the incredible ability to triumph over adversity, and most importantly, she'd had a pure and undying love for her soulmate. Her grandparents' love was the kind most people dreamed of: powerful, unconditional, and inspiring. They were inseparable, often finishing each other's sentences and knowing what the other was thinking without speaking a word. They communicated on a level untapped by most people. Much like she and Rob. Willow was a lot like her grandmother, and for this reason, she knew she would reach Rob one day soon. Their lives were too intertwined to stay apart.

Her cell phone rang, and Willow jumped. "Hello?"

"It's me. Max."

"Hey, Max. What's up?"

"How are you, sweetheart?"

"I'm doing okay."

"Glad to hear it. Listen, I wanted to let you know someone is looking for you. I saw your name on a file in the office today. I asked my associate, Jerry Green, about it. He's handling the investigation."

"Was it Rob?"

"No, he's a young kid. A friend of Jerry's niece. He says your grandmother was his father's teacher. I thought you should know. I think he's harmless. But please be careful. I don't want anything to happen to you."

"Okay. Thanks for telling me. I'll keep my eyes and ears open for anything suspicious."

☯☯☯

It was an unseasonably warm May afternoon, so Chase put on his swim trunks and headed to the park for a dip after school on Wednesday. Although a swim sounded good, he had another, more important motive. He longed to find the girl who'd watched him but then ran away. Who was she, and what did she want? He wanted to know this girl, whoever she was. For some strange reason, he *needed* to know her. It was like a challenge for him, and he intended to speak to her one day.

Chase avoided the crowded beach area and opted for the often-deserted pond, which sat behind an old red and white wooden barn. Many teenagers hung out with their friends, played Frisbee and volleyball, or soaked up the sun's rays. For them, it was a chance to check out the cute girls and guys, flirt a little, and hope someone special would come their way. Chase had no interest in picking up chicks. His thoughts were mostly of Darla, and the mysterious girl who lurked in the park.

He sat on the bench near the pond, skipping rocks and patiently waiting for her. He lingered for hours until dusk settled in and the sun went down. As night crept in, he found it increasingly hard to breathe. He wiped his clammy face and drew in the humid evening air. All around him an eerie mist hung low, like a fascinating scene from a suspense movie. He gazed at the still waters and scanned the woods for signs of life. Other than a few fading bird chirps and an occasional splash of a small fish, no one was around. Where was she?

Chase knew he should leave, but something kept him there. He wasn't ready to give up. *A few more minutes.* He tugged impatiently on his damp shirt and shifted his weight from side to side. His skin felt uncomfortably sticky, and he couldn't stand another moment in his damp clothes. He removed his shirt and dove into the murky waters. It didn't matter what lurked below, the refreshing pond soothed his skin and brought him back to life.

He glided through the water freestyle and relished the peaceful stillness of his environment. Before long, darkness fell over the park, and it was time to be on his way. He swam over to the pond's edge, ready to get out. He froze when he heard a slight rustling among the trees. His gaze darted back and forth as he searched for the source of the noise. An animal? A bird? The wind?

He grinned when he discovered what he had hoped for. There, in the shadows of the early evening, was an image of the girl. He strained to see her.

"Hey," he called. "Come swim with me. The water's nice."

The girl stood there, frozen in place. She stared at him, which sent a wave of excitement coursing through his veins. He had to talk to her.

"C'mon," he said again. "I don't bite."

She shook her head no but still stood there.

"I want to get to know you. And I'm pretty sure you want to get to know me, too. What's your name?"

The girl turned to leave.

"No, wait!" he cried. "Please stay."

She turned her head slightly in his direction, and he began to get out of the water. "Let's talk," he said as he headed her way.

Her eyes grew wide, and she gasped. She took off running.

Chase grabbed his towel and shirt and ran after her. He trailed her and almost caught up when he tripped on a tree root and fell to the ground with a thud. *Ouch!* He brushed himself off and got up, but when he looked around, he saw no one. He had lost her again.

Feeling sad and disappointed, he headed to his car. The thick night air filled his lungs, and he gasped. He couldn't wait to get inside.

As he was about to open the door, an airplane zoomed overhead. His heart thumped, and the fear rose up in his throat like a dense fog rolling in. He braced himself against the side of his car, his head turned upward toward the sky. He watched the plane's red blinking lights as it coasted above and transported him to the terrifying scene that had plagued him for so many years. An inferno of flames engulfed his mind, and he saw himself holding Darla tight, their bodies clenched together in fear. Their last embrace before it all ended.

"I'll always love you," he said.

"I'll always love you, too," she replied. Shattered bits of plane flew around their heads as the heat absorbed their bodies. Then everything faded to black.

"Noo! Darla!" he screamed. "Where are you? I need you."

Chase rested his head against the window of the car door and cried. His sobs echoed through the empty park like a wolf howling at the moon.

He didn't know how long he stood there emptying the contents of his tortured and broken heart. When there were no longer any tears left inside him, he slowly lifted his head and spotted her standing there. Darla looked at him with loving eyes full of compassion and a sad longing. He wanted to run to her and embrace her. He wanted to feel her smooth skin on his. Was he dreaming or was she really there? Had his guardian angel come to rescue him?

Chase blinked hard and tried to focus, but everything became blurry. He closed his eyes for a minute and then reopened them.

Darla was gone.

Was he losing his mind?

CHAPTER 12
OTHERWORLDLY

Dr. Whitgard welcomed Chase with the same bubbly, eccentric greeting at his second appointment on Thursday. "Come, come," he said enthusiastically as his blue eyes lit up with intrigue and wonder.

For a moment, Chase thought he was in the presence of Doc Emmet Brown, an inventor and time traveler from the old sci-fi movie, *Back to the Future*. Dr. Whitgard certainly struck him as a person who was thrilled to discover new things and come up with innovative ways to reach his clients. He also liked to journey into the past, much like Doc Brown.

Chase followed Dr. Whitgard down a short hallway to his office. As he walked through the doors, uneasiness settled in. Not because he felt threatened or intimidated, but rather because he had no idea what to expect or what would come out of today's session.

"Have a seat, my boy," Dr. Whitgard said with a wave of his right arm.

Chase again sat down on the brown leather couch. He nervously scanned his surroundings while fiddling with the blue and green printed throw pillow. Along with the deep brown, earthly furnishings, this time he noticed a small clock in the form of a ship's wheel hanging on the wall directly behind him. Was Dr. Whitgard a sailor? It would certainly make sense, since he loved to travel back in time. Chase could picture the doctor on the open seas, navigating his boat through the rocky waters.

"What are you thinking, Chase?" he asked.

"Do you sail?"

"Why, yes. Yes, I do!" he exclaimed, his face brightening. "Why do you ask?"

"I noticed your clock."

"Of course," he replied as if a light bulb went on inside his head. "The clock was a gift from my late wife."

"I'm sorry."

"Oh, don't be. I rather love the clock. She had good tastes."

"Not about the clock. About your wife."

"My wife? Oh, I do miss her, for sure. But I know we are still connected. This life isn't the end, you know."

"So I've heard," Chase said with a grin.

"You don't believe it?"

"I don't know what to believe anymore."

"Well, then...we'll have to explore the afterlife." He shuffled some papers and took a long sip of his coffee. "Would you like a cup?"

"Sure."

Dr. Whitgard poured Chase a cup from a small pot on a wooden table in the corner of the room. He handed him a mug, which read *Take the Journey*. Chase laughed to himself. He was on a journey, for sure!

"Ready to travel back in time, my boy?"

"Yep. More than ever."

Dr. Whitgard urged Chase to go a bit further this time, dig a bit deeper. He explained that the further back Chase could go, the more likely he was to uncover something to explain his symptoms. No one wanted an explanation and closure more than Chase. This had gone on too long.

Chase took a long sip of his coffee.

"I want you to picture yourself as a baby," Dr. Whitgard instructed.

The coffee went down the wrong way, and Chase began coughing and choking. "What?" he asked, trying to catch his breath.

"You heard me."

"But I have no memory of being a baby. This is silly and useless."

"Trust me, Chase. Give it a try."

"All right then…if you say so," he said reluctantly.

Chase still didn't understand what value trying to see himself as a baby had. It seemed doubtful this process could reveal why he had been having the visions and dreams all these years. But Chase liked Dr. Whitgard, and though the doc was a bit unconventional, he exuded confidence and hope—two things Chase craved.

Chase closed his eyes and breathed deeply. He counted slowly to ten and became acutely aware of his surroundings. Every sensation, every scent. So crisp and clear now. Dr. Whitgard's potent aftershave tickled his nose and reminded him of the kind his grandfather often wore. The nearby coffee maker dripped rhythmically and emitted a powerful aroma. The cool air rushed around him as the ceiling fan whirred above and made a whooshing sound. His senses awakened, and he felt alive and invigorated. He was a part of it all.

But what he noticed most was laughter—an infant's tiny, joyful giggles. He concentrated to see where the sound was coming from. Did Dr. Whitgard have a client who had brought a baby? An infant in a therapy office seemed very unusual.

As he concentrated on the sound, he stared into the blackness of his closed eyelids. Before long, a fuzzy image took form. A baby lay in a crib. He giggled as a woman's arm waved something fluffy in front of his face and then wiggled it on the surface of his belly. He laughed even harder.

Everything came into focus, and Chase spotted a small green dinosaur—the one he'd had since he was a baby. The laughing infant was him! Chase looked at the woman, a much younger version of his mom. She peered down at him and wore a huge, happy grin. Love embraced him. He felt safe and protected and knew nothing in the world could ever hurt him.

A tall man with wavy brown hair and kind eyes came into the room and hugged his mom. Chase couldn't see his face, but he felt familiar.

"Hi, honey," his mother said. "How was your day?"

"It was good," the man replied in his father's compassionate voice. "But nothing compares to being here with you and our son."

Chase started to cry, and his dad picked him up. "Hey, little bud," his father said, bouncing him around. "What have you been up to today?"

Chase gazed up at his father's face with curious infant eyes. He took in his dad's features: his smooth, pale skin; shiny brown eyes; and neatly combed hair. His dad wore simple black dress pants and a blue button-down shirt. His smile brought Chase back to a time and place he had long forgotten—the joyful loving days of his youth. A time when he had two parents and all was right with the world.

Chase tried to tell his dad how much he missed him and how he wished he were still alive, but his mouth only uttered muffled baby gurgles.

"You don't say?" Dad asked with a laugh.

His dad squeezed him tight, and Chase could feel his warm, soft skin against his. Love and admiration poured through him.

Suddenly, a strong burning odor stung Chase's nose. The happy scene went up in flames, and airplane fragments scattered across the ground. The sound of emergency sirens shrieked in the distance. His heart raced, and he screamed.

"No!"

"Chase? Are you okay?" Dr. Whitgard called.

Chase remained frozen in time like a stone statue. He tried to move or say something; however, his body didn't respond. Paralysis gripped him tightly.

"Chase?"

Still no reply.

"Let's bring you out, my boy," he said calmly. "Follow my voice. You're okay."

Dr. Whitgard began counting slowly and loudly. In Chase's mind, he walked a long, dark corridor filled with shadowy images best forgotten: Darla's worried face, dancing flames, the plane's wreckage, his father's grave. A haunting chill in the air gave him the sense he was no longer himself. He shuddered. The hallway reminded him of a cave, cold and clammy. He could even hear the methodic drip of stalactites above him, although he couldn't see them.

He couldn't see much of anything, really. He was lost in a dismal abyss, surrounded by sights and images that had brought him pain over the years. All he could do was journey blindly through the dark halls of his psyche, listening to the soothing sound of Dr. Whitgard's voice. He was Chase's navigator, and Chase his helpless passenger. Where would Chase end up? He really didn't know, and it terrified him.

Voices called out around him, and whispers filtered through the shadows. He couldn't make out what they were saying, although he was sure they spoke of him.

"Chase!" Dr. Whitgard cried. "Can you hear me? Are you okay?"

Chase clenched his hands into tight fists and began walking briskly through the darkness. Pain and suffering tormented him with every step: each memory, each vision gathering together to taunt him. He had to get out of this place.

After several minutes, a flicker of light trickled through a tiny window at the end of the hallway, and it filled him with hope. He could still hear Dr. Whitgard's muffled cries in the distance, but they didn't matter much to him now. He followed his own path, no longer afraid where it might lead. He was ready to face whatever awaited him.

Chase took a deep breath and ran for the window.

Its light became brighter and brighter until he could no longer look at it without shielding his eyes. An abundant energy flowed through him like nothing he had ever experienced. His life force invigorated him and brought with it an unfamiliar calm. He was in charge now. He squinted and peered through the shiny glass. His eyes sprang open; he was fully alert and conscious now. But instead of seeing Dr. Whitgard sitting at his desk, there was someone else.

Shock overcame him as he stared at the image standing plainly before him, as real as his own skin. He blinked several times to make sure he could trust his eyes.

His beloved father stood on the other side of Dr. Whitgard's office door, surrounded by a brilliant white glow. He wore the most radiant smile Chase had ever seen. He appeared to be in his mid-twenties and was so full of life. Chase laughed to himself when he got a good look at his clothing: a wacky white polo shirt covered with blue and green golf clubs and balls. Dad loved to golf and had a goofy sense of humor, so the shirt suited him well.

"Chase," he said. "I'm okay. Please don't let what happened in the past interfere with your future. You're on the right path. Everything will be fine. Trust me. Trust yourself. It is the only way."

As his wise father spoke these reassuring words, love and comfort enveloped Chase, much like his tiny infant self being cuddled and soothed. But could it be true? Was his long lost father really with him?

It felt as if he were. The proof was right in front of him. Chase no longer found himself engaged in a hypnosis session with Dr. Whitgard. Instead, the scene had transformed into a lifelike visit with his father. Every fiber of his being was convinced he had traveled far away in those few short moments, to a place he had never dared visit but always dreamed of. There was only one way to find out.

Chase got up from the couch and swiftly walked through Dr. Whitgard's open door, where his father still stood. On the other side, abundant beauty overwhelmed him—lush green trees; wildflowers in vibrant shades of red, yellow, purple, and pink; crystal clear blue skies, and the most glorious scent he had ever breathed in. Everything was so bright, so crisp, so incredibly beautiful. He felt like Dorothy when she woke up in the glorious world of Oz.

"Where am I?" Chase asked.

His father, still standing in the same spot, hugged him with tears in his eyes. "Welcome home, son."

Chase's heart raced. "Wait a minute. Am I dead?"

"No, son. You're very much alive."

"Then how?"

"It's true you're on the other side. This is the spirit world."

"Am I a spirit?"

"We're all spirits, son. It's our true nature. But unlike me, you are still flesh and blood. You haven't passed yet."

"Is my life in danger?"

"No, your physical life is not in danger. You're visiting the spirit world. Your body remains healthy and well in Dr. Whitgard's office."

"How can I be here then?"

"Sometimes people on Earth can visit the spirit world in their dreams or during altered states of consciousness. Your deep hypnotic state allowed you to journey here to see me."

"So I'm not imagining this?"

"Nope. This is the real deal." He patted Chase affectionately on the shoulder.

"How long can I stay?"

"Only a few minutes. But before you go, I have something very important to tell you."

"Okay."

"Everything you have gone through has prepared you for what's next."

"What do you mean?"

"I can't tell you, son," he said, shrugging. "All I can say is that you need to really trust what's inside of you. Embrace it. Let it become you. Don't let anyone steer you off course. I know this has been a struggle for you, but it's vital you break free from everyone else's needs and expectations. You need to start living for yourself."

"I'll try."

"Please also know my death is only part of what has been holding you back. You can let me go now. You can move on and live your life. I will be here waiting for you and your mother when the time comes. In the meantime, go live the life you were meant to live."

"How do I know when I find it?"

"You'll know because of how you feel."

"You mean, like how I feel about Darla?"

"Sort of. But I want you to do something for me."

"What?"

"Forget about Darla."

"You can't be serious! Why?" Darla had been part of Chase's heart and soul since childhood. It seemed impossible to forget about her.

"I am totally serious," his father said. "Darla is gone. You need to let her go. Otherwise, you may miss what's right in front of you."

"Kaitlyn?"

"I can't give you an answer. Only you know."

"I suppose," Chase said sadly.

Although he didn't want to admit it, he knew Dad was right. Darla had died before he was even born. There was no future with her. His future was with a girl on Earth, someone who didn't appear only in his dreams, but was a part of his life, a part of him. But who?

"The answers will come in time, Chase. No need to worry about the details."

"It's so hard not knowing where my life's headed."

"I know, son. But it's all part of the journey."

"It's so great being here with you, Dad. I miss you

so much—and so does Mom. I wish you were a part of our lives still."

"Oh, but I am." He chuckled and patted Chase on the back. "You don't think I would go away without checking on you from time to time, do you?"

Chase smiled. "No, I guess not."

His father hugged him heartily again. "It's time for you to go back now."

"I love you, Dad."

"I love you too, Chase. And please tell your mom how much I love and miss her."

"You bet."

Chase's eyes became blurry, and his father's image shimmered until it disappeared. He soon found himself once again in Dr. Whitgard's office.

The frazzled doc paced and wrung his hands. He didn't seem to notice Chase had returned.

"Hey, Doc!"

Dr. Whitgard jumped. "Chase, my dear boy! Welcome back! You scared me for a minute there."

"No worries. I was on the other side."

Dr. Whitgard's eyes grew wide, and he clapped his hands in excitement. "Excellent," he said with a huge grin. "I think we had a breakthrough. If my instincts are correct, things should begin falling into place soon."

CHAPTER 13
LOSING HER

Being home in the comfort of his own cozy bedroom was far better than Chase had ever remembered. His session with Dr. Whitgard—and visit to the afterlife—had left him drained and disoriented. He lay on his navy blue comforter, listening to some tunes and trying to chill.

The sunlight added a touch of brightness to his white walls; however, nothing could compare to the vivid landscapes and sights he had seen in his dreams and on the "other side." Somehow being here now felt ordinary by comparison. His only consolation: the opportunity to offer much-needed comfort to his grieving mother. She would be home from work soon, and he couldn't wait to tell her he had visited with Dad.

He tapped his leg to the beat and thought about how his life had changed recently. So much had transpired since he returned home from Panama City. He'd traded time with friends for time in seclusion. He'd begun to follow his own gut and pursue the things he believed would bring him peace and closure. No one understood. No one encouraged his quest. He was met with concerned faces and frowns at nearly every turn. Still, he pressed forward, leaving parts of his old life behind, in favor of something better suited to his true essence.

His loneliness had expanded exponentially, and he now saw himself clearly as an outsider in the real world. He had tried for so long to fit in with his peers, but no matter what he said or did, no one really got him. Kaitlyn had some vague idea of who he really was. Even still, she couldn't truly know without experiencing his life herself. He was an alien who had landed on Earth from some other planet, and he desperately wanted to find his place here.

He started to doze, and shortly afterward his cell phone rang. He thought about not answering it, but when he saw the caller ID, he couldn't ignore the call. It was Kaitlyn.

"Hello?"

"Chase? It's Kate."

"Hey there! What's up?"

"We need to talk." Kaitlyn sounded very serious, and he could tell right away something was wrong.

"Okay. Are you all right?"

"I'll explain everything when you get here."

Before he had a chance to say anything else, the phone clicked. Kaitlyn had hung up. A feeling of dread came over him. Whatever she had to say wasn't good. He feared she was sick or moving far away.

The thought of losing her and never seeing her again was too much to bear. He'd known Kaitlyn since third grade, when she'd moved to Sterling Heights with her family. They'd become instant friends, always playing kickball at recess or climbing the monkey bars together. When they were in junior high, Chase suspected Kaitlyn had a crush on him, but he'd said nothing because he hadn't wanted to ruin their friendship. She'd dated other guys over the years, convinced Chase wasn't interested. But he'd noticed her. He'd watched her change from a little girl into a woman.

In high school, he'd pictured himself with her and thought maybe he should make his move. However, she was rarely available. As a cheerleader, she'd always been in the spotlight, and his football teammates had been quick to snatch her up. No one could help but notice her sweet smile and bouncy blonde curls or the cute little short skirt she'd worn so well. What made her special, however, was her heart. Any guy would have been stupid not to be interested in her. Still, Chase had watched and waited. He hadn't wanted to be a part of her trail of guys. He wanted to be *the* guy.

After Brandon broke up with Kaitlyn their senior year, Chase had known it was now or never. He finally asked her out and, shortly after, they had become a couple. Being with Kate had made him happy and proud, but their attraction wasn't soul stirring like he'd dreamed. He and Kaitlyn were close friends, for sure. But when they crossed the line between friends and lovers, an unexpected distance had emerged between them and an overwhelming emptiness invaded his heart.

He had never wanted to lose their friendship and was so sorry he had hurt her and inadvertently led her on.

He hoped and prayed she was okay. She'd sounded so weird on the phone. Something was definitely up.

As he headed for the door with his keys in hand, Mom walked in.

"Hi, Chase," she said. "Where are you going in such a hurry?"

"Kate's house. She sounded like something was up."

"Oh…" Mom said with a look of surprise. "I always liked her. She's good for you. Did you two get back together?"

"No, Mom. We're friends."

She nodded. "Well, at least you had the sense not to let her go completely."

Chase smiled and flung open the door. "I'm not stupid…Oh, and by the way, Dad says hello and he loves you."

Her eyes widened, and she followed him out onto the front porch. "Another dream?"

"Nope. I visited Dad in the afterlife."

"Chase Alexander. You worry me sometimes. What do you mean by *visited*?"

"Hypnosis. Apparently, it's the gateway to the other side. Ask Dr. Whitgard."

She rolled her eyes. "Are you sure this Dr. Whitgard isn't a quack?"

"Positive."

"Please be careful," she cautioned. "There are a lot of unscrupulous people out there who will take your money and tell you whatever they think you want to hear."

"Don't worry, Mom. I'm fine. I can take care of myself."

"Your father said those same words before he..." Her eyes filled with tears, and she quickly brushed them away.

"Oh, Mom." Chase placed his hand gently on her shoulder. "Dad is okay. Really he is. He looked amazing. So happy and glowing. He said he misses you so much."

"I miss him, too." She stared down at the ground and sobbed.

"You will see him again. And he'll probably be wearing the weird shirt he had on when I visited him."

"What shirt?"

"It was really strange. White with a bunch of funky blue and green golf clubs and balls on it."

Mom gasped. "I gave him that shirt when we were first dating. I haven't seen it in thirty years! How did you know about the shirt, Chase?"

"I didn't. Never saw it before in my life. Today was the first time."

"Hmm. How odd." Mom looked at him with a puzzled expression, her eyes searching for an answer that made sense.

"See. I told you I visited with Dad."

The wrinkles on her forehead faded, and a look of peace and comfort came over her. Mom gazed up at the sky and then at Chase. She smiled the biggest smile he'd seen in a long time.

"Maybe you did," she said. "Maybe you did."

Chase gave her another quick hug. "Bye, Mom.

Love you."

And in a flash, he was off to see what was going on with Kaitlyn and why she sounded so funny on the phone. Change was definitely in the air.

☯☯☯

Was it a mistake to let her go?

Persistent loneliness crippled Chase on the way to Kaitlyn's house. A piece of himself was always missing, but the emptiness had multiplied since he and Kaitlyn broke up. Alone in his car, he wanted so badly to cry. Instead, he choked back the tears and drummed his fingers on his steering wheel. He was a boy on the cusp of manhood. He had to keep it together.

When he reached Kaitlyn's street, he noticed her house appeared strangely quiet. The lights were out, and the driveway was empty. *Everyone must be out right now.* He and Kaitlyn would be alone. Maybe she'd planned it so they could have some privacy. Did she want him back?

He pulled his car into her driveway and shut off the engine and headlights. When he approached the front door, Kaitlyn immediately flung it open. She had been watching for him.

"Hi, Kate." He gave her a big hug.

She pulled back from him and folded her arms.

"What's wrong?"

"Chase, I need to tell you something. It's really important."

"Sure. Anything."

"I know we've been friends for a long time…and I've always enjoyed having you in my life…"

"Me, too."

"There's one problem with all of this."

"You want to get back together?"

"No, Chase," she said sadly. "We've been down that road already, and it doesn't work. *We* don't work."

"So what are you saying?"

"I've cherished our friendship over the years. In many ways, you were the best thing to ever happen to me. You befriended me when I was scared and new to the school. All of the good times we shared are so special to me—the late night talks, school dances and games, swimming, sneaking off under the bleachers for some private time. We've done so much together. We've grown up together. And I would never change a moment of it."

"Me neither."

"But…"

"But what? I don't like the way this is sounding, Kate."

"But…I'm sorry, Chase…I can no longer have you in my life," she stammered. Tears flooded her eyes.

"What? What do you mean? We're best friends." His stomach churned, and a sharp pain pierced his chest. He looked pleadingly at Kaitlyn as tears streamed down her face.

She struggled to speak. "We *were* best friends. Things are different now."

"I'm so sorry I hurt you, Kate. It had nothing to do with you. You mean the world to me. I'm trying to get my life sorted out…I'm trying to find myself…We'll always be friends."

Kaitlyn carefully wiped tears and smeary makeup streaks from her face. Then she sat down on the oversized gray sectional and closed her eyes. Chase sat down next to her, and soon she opened her eyes and sighed deeply.

"No, Chase. I can't be your friend anymore because…because…" She burst into tears again. "It hurts too much."

"No, Kaitlyn! Please don't do this. It doesn't have to be this way."

"I'm sorry, it does."

"But we've always had a great friendship. It's been the best. I know things have been tough lately. But I don't want to lose you."

"We *had* an amazing friendship," she agreed. "We can never go back to the way we were. On some level, you know it, too. So much has changed now. I fell in love with you."

"I don't want this, Kate. Please don't cut me out of your life."

She wiped a tear and swallowed. "I'm dating someone else now."

Chase looked down at his feet and then back at her. "Are you happy with this guy?"

"Yes, I am." She wiped her eyes again and smiled. "In fact, we're a couple now. I already told you he asked me to prom."

"Great, Kate," he lied.

"Yes. It is great…Kyle is pretty amazing."

Kyle? Chase's heart sank. "You and Kyle?"

A strange feeling came over Chase as he thought about Kyle and Kaitlyn together. Picturing them kissing made him sick to his stomach. "How could you and Kyle do this to me? We're all supposed to be friends!"

"You're the one who gave me up. I'm simply moving on."

"With one of my best friends?"

"Like I said, Kyle's an awesome guy."

"I know, but friends aren't supposed to date your exes." Chase's face became hot with jealously and anger. "It's wrong!" he exclaimed, raising his voice. "Kyle had no right to swoop in and make you his as soon as we were done! That's not friendship; it's betrayal."

"Please don't be upset. This is for the best." She grabbed his hand. He quickly pulled it away and turned to leave. But before he did, he turned back to Kaitlyn.

"I hate you! And Kyle, too! You two deserve each other."

He slammed the door and walked out of her life. His best friend, the girl he had always counted on, was gone for good. He pulled his cell phone out of his pocket and dialed Kyle's number.

Kyle answered right away. "Hey, bud."

"Don't 'hey bud' me, you piece of trash! You're such a jerk. I can't believe you would snatch Kaitlyn up the minute I turned my back."

"Dude, calm down. You broke up with her, remember?"

"Of course I remember, you dirt bag! But you know how I feel about her. Kate is special to me. You're treading on my turf here. Friends don't take a friend's girlfriend away."

"She's not your girlfriend anymore," Kyle said angrily. "Get a life."

"Oh, I have a life and I intend to live it. Don't expect it to ever include you again. Or her. I hate you both."

Chase pushed the call end button and threw his phone to the ground. The cracked screen reflected the moonlight's watchful glint and triggered a wave of emotion as powerful as a tsunami crashing against him. He sobbed. Deep, throaty sobs.

They intensified, and he fell to the ground in a heap. He was no longer almost a man; he was an injured boy. He could no longer hold back the emotions brewing deep inside of him. Like a waterfall, tears rushed down his face and soaked his sweatshirt. He couldn't believe he had lost both of his best friends. Life would never be the same. Why must he suffer over and over again? Why couldn't he have a normal life like everyone else?

He continued to sob until he heard a girl's voice call from behind him.

"Are you okay?"

He sat up and turned to look. The mysterious girl from the park stood over him. She looked as beautiful as an angel with her brown hair glimmering in the moonlight and her concerned eyes peering down at him. Somehow this stranger brought him peace. He had a sudden urge to reach out and hug her, but he held back. Instead, he rose shakily and wiped his face on his shirt sleeve.

"I'm okay now. You're here. Can we talk?"

She smiled briefly, then nodded. "I'm sorry about the other night. When I ran away."

"You don't need to apologize. You know what they say—don't talk to strangers." He chucked. "For all you know, I could be an ax murderer or something."

She ran her hand through her hair and tilted her head. "I know that's not true. Besides, you're not a stranger."

"Oh, since you've stalked me a few times, I seem familiar to you now, huh?"

She smiled and touched his shoulder. An unexpected flutter stirred within him. She was flirting, and he liked it.

"No, really," she said. "I think we might know each other from long ago."

Chase studied her carefully—her playful smile and exuberant inner glow—but no names or details came to mind. He guessed she was in her twenties. She did seem strangely familiar and appeared certain she knew him, but he couldn't place her. She must have noticed the perplexed look on his face.

"You don't recognize me?" she asked.

"Umm…well sort of…you're the girl who keeps following me." He felt bad he had no idea who she was and wasn't sure what else to say.

"It's okay. I'm so happy to finally see you again. I've really missed you."

"I'm happy to see you, too," Chase said, which wasn't a lie because he felt a strange attraction between them. Besides, he had grown tired of chasing her down and was glad to finally talk to her face to face.

Standing so close to her made him take notice of her beauty and charm. Her brown hair was shoulder length and straight, but what drew him in were her eyes—deep brown and full of passion and wonder. He almost recognized her. Where had he seen her before?

A flash of Darla appeared in his head. *Of course, she reminded him of Darla!* Without thinking, he leaned in and kissed her passionately. She returned his kiss with equal fervor.

When they pulled apart, she flashed him a huge, happy smile. "You do remember me! Now we can finally be together again."

Chase's eyes widened. "Together?"

"I know it's been a while, but the way you kissed me says you still love me. Surely, you must remember what we once shared."

"I'm sorry. I don't remember anything."

"But your eyes…and your smile…they don't lie. You must be him."

"Who?"

"You were my first and only true love."

"Wait a minute…not so fast…You must have confused me with someone else."

"Really? I was so sure you were him."

"Nope. I'm only seventeen. I haven't had much time to fall in love yet. If we were a couple, I would remember."

A tear slid down her cheek, and her lower lip quivered. Chase's heart raced, and he didn't know if he should walk away or kiss her again. Something about this girl drew him to her. When she looked at him with her beautiful brown eyes, his mind journeyed to a place he'd only seen in his dreams. A place where he was in love, and the emptiness he often felt vanished. But she was a complete stranger. How could he feel this way about her?

"I'm sorry I bothered you," she said, turning to leave.

As she headed down the street past Kaitlyn's house, Chase scrambled after her. He didn't want her to go away when he still longed to know her better. He walked briskly past the neat row of brick and vinyl sided houses, each with a maple tree in front at the curb. The girl's pace quickened as she looked at him over her shoulder.

"Please wait," he cried.

She darted across the street in front of a car, and he flinched as the horn blared. She quickly disappeared into a neighbor's yard. Chase followed, scanning the yard for signs of her. He looked behind the brown wooden shed and around the other side of the spruce trees. He walked past the empty in-ground pool to the gazebo and around to the opposite side of the house. There was no sign of her.

Who was this girl and why was he so drawn to her? Did he really know her, perhaps from his childhood?

There was only one way to find out. He pulled his cell phone from his pocket and dialed Jerry Green. "Mr. Green. This is Chase. There's a girl who keeps following me. I need to find out who she is."

CHAPTER 14
SHATTERED DREAMS

Loss had followed Chase everywhere, from the time he was a young boy. First, his father, then his dream girl, and now Kate and Kyle. Even the girl from the park had run away from him, despite the mutual attraction they shared.

But the biggest loss of all was himself. He struggled to make sense of the world around him and find his place. No matter how hard he tried, obstacles stood in his way. Why was life so hard? Why did nothing feel right?

Chase lay awake in bed, staring at the ceiling. His restless, weary mind raced with thoughts of the past and future. A confusing, jumbled mass expanded in his head. To make matters worse, conflict, and the growing emptiness inside, pushed him further and further away from his friends and family, as well as all he had come to know and expect.

He tried counting sheep and got to 2,000. He stared at the insides of his eyelids until they turned as black as the night sky. He tossed and turned for what seemed like hours, never knowing what he needed to quiet his mind and restore his hope. Getting some shuteye seemed nearly impossible under these conditions, and finding what he needed to feel whole and complete was even more elusive.

Until she came to him again. It was as if she knew he needed her.

Darla reached out her hand, and he willingly took it. She was absolutely gorgeous and glowing, the picture of an angel who had come to save him. She wore an elegant red lace dress and matching lipstick. Mounds of delicate brown curls rested on her head in a sophisticated up-do. She smiled at him lovingly, which made him believe everything would be okay. She might not be alive on Earth, but she knew exactly how to rescue him. She guided him by the hand to the dance floor.

They must be at a prom. Chase scanned the room, taking in the sights and sounds around him. Red and white balloons hung over the dance floor in a flowing cascade, and tiny, colored lights flashed in sync with the music. Enthusiastic teenagers swayed to the songs and celebrated their final high school days. The DJ played the best tunes, while many sang along or tapped their feet to the booming beat. Chase couldn't help but sing, too. He spun Darla around, and she giggled with delight.

Their bodies brushed against each other as they thumped and wiggled to the rhythm. The tension between them slowly built like a drum roll, and he ached for more of her. When a slow song came on, he held her close and relished the sensation of her warm breath on his neck. His heart pounded with excitement. Being with Darla was a thrill unlike any other. He came alive when he was with her. He was his true self.

"Darla," he said softly.

She lifted her head to look up into his eyes. Her beautiful brown eyes held such compassion and depth. He couldn't imagine anyone more stunning. "I love you," he said, brushing her cheek gently with his fingertips.

"I love you, too."

Chase leaned in and kissed her; their lips glided effortlessly together. They seemed to melt right into each other. Everything was perfect. He wanted to stay forever by her side.

"Darla. Please don't ever leave me," he begged.

She looked away with a hint of sadness. "I can't promise you. But no matter what happens, love will always find a way."

Chase pulled away from her and clutched his chest, which now ached with emptiness.

This isn't reality. It's only a dream. *They could never really be together because she was already dead.*

Chase suddenly understood exactly how Kaitlyn felt. Being his friend wasn't enough for her. Her heart yearned for more of him, like his heart longed for more of Darla. It was an impossible dream with no real solution. He was trapped in some useless fantasy world.

His chest constricted, and he drew in a sharp breath. He knew what he had to do. "I'm sorry, Darla. A fantasy isn't good enough for me. I deserve more...a real relationship with a real person."

She raised her eyebrows and gave him a troubled look. "So what are you saying?"

"I can't see you anymore. I need to let you go. It hurts too much to be with you when I know we can never have anything more than this."

"You're being ridiculous. After all we've been through, do you really want to give up on our love?"

"This isn't love. Love is something between two people—two living, breathing people. This is fake."

"Well, if that's how you see it, then I guess there's nothing left to say." She folded her arms across her chest and scanned Chase's face. Did she expect him to hang onto her at any cost?

He could no longer keep up the charade. His dad was right; it was time to move on and live the life he was meant to live, whatever it was.

"Good-bye, Darla."

A tear slid down Darla's face, and she quickly wiped it away with her finger. "Good-bye, my love."

Then she turned away from him and shimmered into the air, leaving behind a misty trail of sparkles and his shattered heart.

CHAPTER 15
ON HIS OWN

Chase awoke with a pounding headache. His stomach churned, and he wanted to throw up. He didn't think it was possible to feel any more alone. He now had nothing and no one to share his life with. The emptiness crushed down on his chest, and he could hardly breathe. He had to get some air.

He threw on some clothes and sped to the park, with windows down and his hair rippling unpredictably in the wind. The sights around him seemed dim and out of focus. Cars whirred in fuzzy blobs, and even the sun had lost its luster. When he reached the park, he breathed a sigh of relief. He was safe here.

He jumped out of his car and headed for the trails. At least he still had them.

He absentmindedly grabbed a stick from the ground and began fiddling with it. A familiar giggle brought his attention to the path's edge. A young couple ran their hands up and down each other's backs and kissed profusely. *Oh no. Kate and Kyle.*

A blade pierced through his heart, and he wanted so badly to punch the jerk. But violence wasn't the answer. *Keep it together. Don't make things worse. You've already hurt Kate enough.*

He gripped the stick tight and broke it in half. Something inside him snapped, and a flow of emotions rose to the surface. He held his breath and fought back tears as he turned to walk away. He had never wanted or intended for Kaitlyn to be out of his life. She had always been there, and he'd assumed she always would be. Now he felt so misguided and naïve.

Had he made a mistake by breaking up with her? Now that they were no longer a couple and she was with Kyle, he wanted so badly to be with her again. Despite all of the confusion, Kaitlyn was still special to him. She was the girl who believed in him and cheered him on through every challenge and accomplishment. She was real. Living, breathing, flesh and blood—unlike Darla. But he had given her up. He'd traded her for an impossible dream, and now she was no longer a part of his life. What had he done?

"Hey, Chase!" a girl's voice called.

He turned and saw Ashley approaching him, her brown hair bouncing.

"I haven't seen you in a while."

"Hi, Ash. How's it going?"

"Good. I bought my prom dress. Joe's taking me."

"Cool. I still can't believe you two are seeing

each other."

"Well, we're not exclusive or anything. Joe made it very clear he wants to date other girls while he's away at college. But you never know. We'll see where things go."

"Sounds like the smart thing to do."

"Yeah. Missed you at the senior all-night party. Where were you?"

"Didn't feel like going."

Ashley frowned and narrowed her eyes. "Want some advice?"

Chase shrugged. "Not really."

"Well, too bad, cuz you need to hear this."

His eyes widened. "Okay. Whatever."

She leaned forward and raised her eyebrows. "You can't drop out of life, Chase. It doesn't solve anything."

"I'm not dropping out. I'm trying to find myself, my place."

Ashley shook her head. "You already have your place," she said, raising her voice. "It's in college, going after the career you've worked hard for and deserve. It's with your friends and family."

"You're wrong. Nothing feels right in my life. Something's missing. I need to find out what it is."

"Well, as long as you stop living, something will always be missing. Don't lose sight of what's important."

"Don't worry. I've got this."

"Okay. If you say so...Anyway, are ya ready for prom?"

"No. I'm not going."

"Seriously? I thought you and Kaitlyn were supposed to go together."

"Nope. After we broke up, she decided not to go with me."

"Oh, I'm sorry. I didn't know." She tilted her head and gawked at him sadly. Then her face brightened. "I have an idea! You can go with Mary Beth. She's a really nice girl…smart, too…and she doesn't have a date…I'll call her right now." She pulled out her phone and started to dial.

Chase grabbed her phone and hit the end call button.

"No, Ash," he said firmly. "I'm *not* going. I don't wanna go to prom with Mary Beth…Kaitlyn…or anyone."

"Sorry. You don't have to get so bent out of shape."

Chase thought of Darla and their romantic dance at the prom in his dream. He missed her more than ever now. He had no girlfriend, no dreams to look forward to, and no future plans. His life was an empty ball of nothingness. How would he ever fill the void inside him?

"Sorry. I'm a little on edge lately."

"I've noticed. What's up with you?"

"Don't know."

Joe walked up to join them. "Hey there!" He wrapped his arms around Ashley and gave her a squeeze before looking at Chase. "What's going on?"

"Nothing."

"No offense. But you look awful, dude. Like you got hit by a truck or something. What the heck happened to you?"

Chase did feel pretty crappy. His eyes burned from lack of sleep, and his mind was in a fog. A numbness now shielded him from the intense emotions threatening to destroy him. He was hopelessly lost and alone.

"I'm all right, man," he replied.

"So what's with Kaitlyn?" Joe asked.

"What do you mean?"

"I saw her making out with Kyle!"

"Yeah. She's with him now."

"No way! Aren't you going to do something, dude?"

"Nope. It's her life. Besides, she doesn't want to be friends with me anymore."

Joe threw his hands in the air. "Are you wimping out, man? It's so not like you."

"I'm not wimping out. I'm moving on."

"What? You two were inseparable," said Ashley. "How can you stand there and do nothing? And how can she cut you out of her life?"

"I asked myself the same question. Why did she end our friendship? It didn't make sense. Then I had a dream last night. It really gelled things for me. She says it's too painful to be with me if we're not a couple. She wants it all or nothing. I get it now. It's torture to be around someone you love and not be able to be with them."

"Are you talking about your silly dream girl again, Chase?" Ashley asked.

"I am."

She shook her head disapprovingly. "You really need to let her go. Lusting after some impossible fantasy isn't healthy. You had a good thing with Kaitlyn, and you blew it. How much more do you have to lose before you come to your senses?"

"I know I can never have Darla. I've decided to put her behind me."

"Good. Now you can focus on college and your future." She put a hand on her hip. "So do you have your classes picked out?"

"Nope. I don't think I wanna go to college right now."

Ashley's eyes grew wide with concern and her face turned red. "What? You're dropping out of college, too? What's wrong with you? Besides, you're supposed to room with Joe!"

"Yeah, man," Joe agreed. "You can't ditch me!"

"Do you really think not going will solve all your problems?" Ashley asked.

He had problems all right. Where was this bright future his father had hinted at? His dad had seemed so certain he was on the right path, but what did Dad really know? After all, he was dead, too, like Darla.

Chase didn't know much at this point, but one thing was clear: All his life he had avoided responsibility for his future and had been a pawn in everyone else's game. When he'd attempted to seize his own destiny recently, it felt empowering but led nowhere. His friends thought he was crazy. It would be so easy right now to give up and put his fate in someone else's hands again. He could simply go back to his old behavior patterns—listening to and agreeing with what everyone else saw for him. He felt the pull toward that life. It was what he knew best. The way he'd always been. But the pull to be himself and find his own way was even stronger.

Despite being urged to go to MSU and study chemistry, Chase was adamant in his decision to take a break from school for a while. What good was a future he wasn't passionate about? Whatever he chose to do with his life, it had to mean something to *him*, not everyone else.

His soul-searching had led him to conclude there was something bigger, something more he'd been missing all these years. Once he located the missing pieces, he truly believed his life would transform. He would never forget about Darla or give up on finding answers to his past. He would continue to pursue regression therapy with Dr. Whitgard. He would head to the park in search of the intriguing girl who thought she knew him. The incredible kiss they'd shared made him realize he could actually have the love and passion he had experienced in his dreams. And if nothing else, maybe he would find a new friend or rediscover an old one. He had to see this through to the end, wherever it led. His gut told him it was the right choice.

"I don't know, Ash," he said. "But I've been living for everyone else far too long. It's time I lived for me, for a change. I need to find myself."

Joe shook his head. "I never pegged you for a screw up, dude. What's gotten into you? Have the psychics messed with your head? I told you voodoo was no good. But you didn't listen to me. You're such a chump."

"Chase, honey, please reconsider this college thing," Ashley urged. "Don't throw away your future."

"Yeah, man. Even I'm going to college. And you

know what I partier I am. Gotta get your priorities straight."

"I am. I've been seeing a hypnotherapist named Dr. Whitgard," Chase said defensively. "I think he can help me."

Joe laughed. "Now I've heard everything! Psychics. Dropping out of school. Hypnosis. Don't be a loser, Chase. Stay away from those weirdos and get your crap together. Before it's too late."

Ashley put her hand on Chase's shoulder. "Joe's right. You really need to get your life on track. You're a smart guy with a bright future. This is the most exciting time of your life. Don't blow it."

An uncomfortable heat flushed Chase's cheeks. They were supposed to be his friends. How dare they criticize his choices? He'd worked so hard lately to figure things out. Didn't they care what he was going through? This was the last straw.

He sucked in air through his mouth and raised his shoulders. "I thought you guys were my friends," he yelled. "But all you seem to do is tell me what to do. You never accept the person I really am. I don't need this crap from you or anyone!"

"Chase honey, we are your friends," Ashley said. Her condescending tone sounded more like a parent talking to a small child, and it angered him.

Chase glanced at his shattered iPhone. *Oh crap. I'm gonna to be late for my appointment.* He planted his feet firmly in the ground and looked from Ashley to Joe. The only way to find himself was to let go. "I don't need either of you," he shouted. "Stay the hell out of my life!"

Chase ran down to his car and slid into his seat. As he started to pull away, he noticed several park visitors staring at him. Some were classmates from school or his neighborhood. They weren't only watching him; they pitied him. They felt sorry for him.

Their behavior could only mean one thing—they knew.

The whole neighborhood knew he and Kaitlyn were no longer friends and Kyle was her new guy. They probably even overheard his outburst at Joe and Ashley. How humiliating! And now he was left with nothing—no girlfriend, no friends, no future. He had lost it all.

He wanted to squeal his tires and get the heck out of there. Somehow, he kept his cool.

As he started the car, Kaitlyn and Kyle got into the truck next to him. He ignored them. They were no longer a part of his life. He was on his own now. He'd risked it all to follow his gut.

Then it hit him: He was truly free. Nothing or no one would stand in his way now.

Coming to this realization brought him an enormous sense of liberation. The cage door had opened, and he had flown out.

Chase pointed his car toward Dr. Whitgard's office with fierce determination. Something life-altering was on the verge. He could feel it.

CHAPTER 16
INTO THE DARKNESS

"Darla came to me again," Chase said, as he sat in the brown leather chair in Dr. Whitgard's office.

"Oh, she did?" Dr. Whitgard ran his fingers through his long bushy beard. "And what did she say?"

"It's more like what I said."

"What did you say, Chase?"

"We were at the prom, dancing. I could feel our love—it was incredible. We kissed. Then, I asked her never to leave me, and she said she couldn't promise anything. So, I ended things."

Dr. Whitgard coughed hard and cleared his throat. "What? You ended your relationship with the love of your life?"

"She can't be the love of my life, Doc. She never really was. I'm tired of chasing after some out-of-reach fantasy with a ghost. I told her I couldn't see her anymore because our relationship wasn't real, and I wanted more. My dad's right. I need to let her go so I can get on with my real life."

"Hmmm. This is all quite interesting." He looked at Chase with his kind blue eyes and nodded his head repeatedly.

"Well, what do you think it means, doc?"

"I can't be sure, but it's possible this means you are putting the past behind you, like your father suggested. Maybe you're finally healing from the trauma of his tragic accident and death."

"Do you think the visions will stop?"

"They might. But we still need to get to the bottom of why Darla has been in your visions and dreams to begin with."

"Well, I thought we already knew the answer. It's because Darla was my guardian angel. Maybe my dad sent her to watch over me."

"People typically don't have romantic relationships with their guardian angels, Chase. Your case is highly peculiar. I suspect there is more to all of this. I intend to find out what it is."

"How, Doc?"

"With more hypnosis, of course."

"Where are we going this time?"

"We're going back to a time before time."

"I don't understand."

"Oh, you will, my boy," He chuckled. "You will."

Chase closed his eyes and let Dr. Whitgard guide him to his destination. He followed the doctor's melodic voice and the mesmerizing flute music back to a place deep within his subconscious, a place he had never dared to travel. He sat in the back of a classroom, alongside his dad. Mrs. Darla Chambers stood at the chalkboard.

Next, he waved good-bye as his father boarded a private plane. Soon after, he found himself inside his father's plane as a young boy. He bounced happily in his seat, which was directly behind his mother's. He looked down at his lap and adjusted a seatbelt. He now prepared for a crucial journey of his own. Dr. Whitgard was the trusty pilot, and he was his passenger. Only this time, he hoped it wouldn't end in a fatal crash.

Dr. Whitgard instructed Chase to go back to the time when he was an infant. The scene came quickly and easily and was as Chase had remembered it last time. The same bubbly sense of awe, love, safety, and security ran through his body. His parents were so happy, and so was he. Only this time, he didn't try so hard to talk to his dad. He knew this was a memory and not the real thing.

Next, the doc urged him to focus on the baby and imagine himself in the womb before his mother gave birth. Within minutes, the images of his parents faded, and he found himself surrounded by blackness.

"It's all dark."

"What do you hear?" Dr. Whitgard asked.

"Nothing."

"Do you see anything else? Concentrate, Chase. Describe for me everything you feel and notice."

"There's a problem. I feel nothing. I hear nothing. I see nothing. It's as if I don't even exist."

"Hmm."

"What else do you want me to do?"

"Keep concentrating. Think of a time before you were conceived. When you were a twinkle in your parents' eyes."

"Okay," he said, feeling frustrated.

Chase stared deep into the blackness, intent on unveiling some long-forgotten secret trapped inside his psyche. The darkness pulled him in and absorbed him like a black hole. A lonely, empty space encased him—soundless, weightless, and without light. He soon fell into a vast and expanding nothingness, an unending infinite pool with no escape. The images he fought to visualize never materialized. His father didn't appear before him to offer comfort and encouragement. Darla didn't come to rescue him or profess her undying love. Not a single airplane flew by, crashed, or went up in flames. It was all gone. Everything he had carried with him had suddenly vanished without a trace.

"Anything now?" Dr. Whitgard asked.

"No. Nothing."

"Are you sure?"

"Yes. Everything's still black. I don't see anything. It's like I'm in a dark, empty closet, all alone. There's no one here. I don't even know if I'm here. What am I supposed to see, anyway?"

"There is no supposed to. What you see depends on you."

"Well, I guess I'm empty then. Empty and alone."

"I'm sorry, Chase. We'll try again another time. I want you to go home and get some rest."

Tears welled up in Chase's eyes. He didn't bother to wipe them or hide them. He had no reason to. All this work had led to only one conclusion: he was truly lost. Would he ever find his way?

Chase's solemn and confused state led him once again to Lincoln Park. A persistent emptiness flooded his mind and heart, and escape was nowhere in sight. His last session with Dr. Whitgard was so disappointing. He had expected his hypnotherapy appointments to reach a culmination and finally shed light on the issues that had plagued him since early childhood. But what he was left with instead was absolutely nothing.

He still didn't fully understand the romantic dreams and fantasies of Darla and began to doubt he ever would. Even more disturbing was the fact that he was no closer to understanding himself. Dr. Whitgard had tried to take him to a time before he was born, and his approach had failed miserably. Being in the blackness only left him feeling more lonely than ever. Like an astronaut, stranded in outer space after his line had been severed. He had no idea where his ship was and had no way of getting back to his crewmates. He didn't know what Dr. Whitgard expected him to see since he hadn't existed back then anyway. He guessed the doc had some weird theory about him being able to view events from his father's past or something. Whatever it was, it didn't work, and Chase had lost all hope.

He couldn't believe he had put so much trust in Dr. Whitgard's judgment and had counted on being led to some sort of closure or epiphany. His gut had told him time and time again he was on the right track. Now he wondered if he had been mistaken. How could he have been so wrong?

As he drove the familiar path to his destination, he reflected on recent events and the direction his life had taken. Maybe his friends, mother, and teachers were right after all. Perhaps it was time to throw in the towel, go off to college, and give up on hypnotherapy, psychics, private investigators, and messages from beyond. He felt so defeated, so hopeless. His life and visions had lost all meaning. He had expended all this effort to find himself; for what? Nothing. The park was all he had now.

When Chase arrived at the park, it was right before dusk. The sun had begun to set and a quiet stillness took over the air. Visitors were scarce, so it was the perfect setting for him to think. He headed down the gravel path that traveled through the woods. The trail was about one mile long, and when he reached the end, it opened up into a large clearing with a stunning pond. Sometimes he would fish there; other times he would sit and enjoy nature. Being outdoors in this tranquil setting soothed him. Once he left his car, he entered another world, a private place where he could reconnect with who he was and leave the worries and troubles of his hectic existence behind.

He desperately needed some solace tonight. The park was his only hope. His friends, his girlfriend, his dream girl, his therapist—they had all let him down. He really had no idea what was next. His past was fuzzy; his future unattainable. Why had he ever been given the chance to know Darla at all? Why had he gotten a taste of love, only to have it taken away?

Think, Chase, think. Find a new plan. This can't be how the quest ends.

It was a longshot, but there was one last thing he could do. He would call Jerry Green again. The private investigator had never called back with Darla's granddaughter's address, and Chase was tired of waiting. He dialed the number and Mr. Green answered right away.

"Hello, Chase."

"Hi, Mr. Green. Do you have any information for me?"

"Oh, I'm sorry I didn't get back to you sooner. I was tied up with another case and spent the last week out of the country. Hang on a minute, and I'll get you the address."

"Okay. Thanks."

Mr. Green returned in a few minutes with an address for Darla's granddaughter, Willow. Anticipation ran through Chase's body. This was his last shot.

"Any news on who's been following me?"

"Afraid not. I've been too busy to do any digging."

"No problem. Thanks for the address, Mr. Green."

"You're welcome. Good luck, Chase."

Chase hung up the phone and headed further down the park trail. The shuffling of his feet against the earth and the chirping of birds were the only sounds he could hear now as he traveled deeper into the woods.

He thought more about Darla and wondered why she'd been with him since childhood. Was she really an angel sent to comfort and guide him? Was there some significance to her being his father's teacher? Was it all a fluke? Or could it be some sort of cosmic anomaly, a gift Chase had been given to see the past and envision a life with someone he had never met? As a child, he had always enjoyed puzzles, but he found it difficult to fit the missing pieces of this one together. Even Dr. Whitgard had been unable to offer concrete answers.

Chase inhaled the warm spring air as he reached the path's end and headed to his favorite pond. The sun had sunk down into the horizon, and darkness had begun to settle on the earth. He grabbed a stone from the bumpy ground below and skipped it across the still waters. His gaze fixed on the ripples projecting out from where the stone had landed. He watched until they slowly faded, and then quickly tossed another stone. He did this again and again until it was too dark to see. Then he looked up from the water and decided he'd better head back to the entrance before he could no longer see anything at all.

As he turned to leave, he once again spotted a hazy figure of a girl standing on the trail. He didn't get his hopes up this time. Although she'd been watching him for quite some time, he now knew she'd mistaken him for someone else. He had lost her, too. Maybe he was one of those people who was always losing someone or something. Perhaps he was perpetually lost himself.

He continued to watch the girl. She didn't move. He walked toward her a bit, and she waved excitedly, motioning him over. He shrugged his shoulders. She motioned again, so he headed to the path to see what she wanted.

As Chase approached her, she ran to him with a huge smile on her face.

"I'm so glad to see you!" She threw her arms around him and planted a big wet kiss on his cheek.

How odd. What's up with this chick?

"You know I'm not your long lost love, so why are you still following me?" he asked.

She gulped. "I…I…don't know. I thought you felt it, too. You know, the electricity between us."

It was true. He did feel something. He wasn't sure if it was because he was attracted to her or because she reminded him of Darla. Whatever the case, it was hardly enough to build a relationship on. He'd spent far too long chasing useless fantasies. Darla was no more.

He ached for her now from the very depths of his soul. He wanted to be with her more than ever. He longed for a limitless love that made his heart thump and his knees shake. Was he crazy?

Without thinking, he leaned over and kissed the girl.

"You do remember me!" she exclaimed happily.

"Um…I'm sorry. I was so out of line. I really don't remember you. The truth is I wanted to kiss you again."

He thought she would be angry. He even expected she might slap him across the face and leave. What kind of a jerk was he to kiss a stranger?

Surprisingly, she had no objections. Instead, she smiled mischievously and kissed him passionately. Their kiss stirred Chase's soul. It escalated quickly, and soon he found himself running his hands through her hair and down her body as she did the same to him. He trembled with hunger, and never wanted to leave her side.

They pulled apart breathlessly, gazing helplessly into each other's eyes. Chase did know her somehow; he could feel it. He searched her face in a desperate attempt to recognize her. Was she a long forgotten childhood friend? He still couldn't place her.

She looked down at the ground as if he had admitted it aloud. "I can't believe you forgot about me."

"So, you said I was your first and only true love. What did you mean? Were we childhood friends?"

"No, we were lovers."

"As I said, I'm only seventeen. I would remember if we were lovers."

"You've lived far longer than seventeen years."

"Huh? You're not making any sense."

"It's like I told you before, love will always find a way."

"What? You never said those words to me. You're confusing me."

"Well, let me make it simple for you. You're my husband…from another life."

Dread came over Chase. She was sexy, beautiful, and *crazy*. He wanted her so badly, but he couldn't get involved with someone who had lost touch with reality. He needed to be grounded. He'd spent far too long with his head in the clouds.

"I'm sorry. I can't listen to this nonsense," he said.

"It's true." She smiled and leaned in to kiss him.

He smelled her perfume, which hinted of roses. His heart fluttered, and his knees grew weak. Every fiber of his being wanted to take her in his arms, kiss her passionately, and never let her go. But he knew better.

He took a step back, and she opened her eyes with a look of disappointment.

“Find someone else to play your games with,” he said. “I won’t be yours or anyone else’s pawn.”

She stared at him, as if she were waiting for something. He turned and walked away into the darkness of the night.

CHAPTER 17
CONNECTED

Willow drank coffee at the kitchen table early Saturday morning. She still wore her fuzzy blue pajamas and contemplated not getting dressed. What was the point? She had no family left, and Rob still wasn't a part of her life. She wondered if he ever would be. She ached for him to love her the way he once had. Since he'd deserted her in the park, a cloud of melancholy had surrounded her. Why weren't things the way they should be?

The doorbell's loud buzz startled her. *Who could it be?*

She got up from her seat and peered through the tiny peephole.

Her heart fluttered as she saw him on her doorstep, as handsome as ever. She almost couldn't believe Rob stood right in front of her. He had found her! She could still feel the magical, passionate kiss they'd shared in the park the other night. Waves of tingling electricity rippled through her body. Their kiss must have finally triggered a memory for him, and he had come to be with her. She'd prayed so long for this and couldn't wait to pick up where they had left off all those years ago.

She hadn't wanted to pressure him into remembering who she was. She had thought it much better for him to realize everything on his own. It was the only way she could be sure their connection was still strong. She knew he was attracted to her, but wasn't satisfied with a relationship built on lust. She wanted his whole heart and soul. She needed all of him.

Willow looked down at her fluffy pajamas and sighed. She couldn't let him see her like this. She was such a mess, hardly the beautiful young girl he had fallen in love with back then. She hadn't even brushed her teeth or combed her hair. As much as she ached to fling open the door and fall into his arms, their reunion would have to wait. Now that he remembered, he would come back to see her another time. She was sure of it.

Next time, she would be ready.

He knocked again.

She stared through the peephole, taking in his endearing features. His gorgeous brown eyes seemed to be looking right at her, as if he sensed she was only inches away from him. She could feel the energy of his love; their passion still burned brightly and always would. The thought of them being together again sent tingles through her entire body and made her tremble with anticipation. So much so that she almost opened the door and pulled him inside.

She imagined them on the couch, wrapped in each

other's arms, kissing intensely. They would never let each other go again. Once they were back together, nothing could stand in their way. Their love was much too powerful, much too enduring.

After a few minutes, he turned and walked away, his head hung in disappointment.

"A little bit longer, my love," she said softly. "Then we will be together."

Rob glanced back over his shoulder at her, appearing to have heard the words she spoke. Then he headed for the parking lot and disappeared.

Chase put on his cap and gown and glanced at himself in the mirror. He looked very put together for someone who was so out of sorts. His visit to Willow's house earlier had been a dead end, and he was left once again empty-handed. A quiet sadness fell upon him, and he wondered if he would ever find the answers he sought. It certainly wasn't for lack of trying.

In the past month, he had taken some pretty drastic steps and made changes in his life he thought would lead him to the truth. Although he had gotten closer, he still had no closure. The peace he'd been searching for his whole life had eluded him. Now he must join his graduating class and face his uncertain future. He'd reached his lowest point, more alone and sad than he had ever felt in his life. He'd once thought he was on the cusp of something big, but no clear picture of where he was headed had emerged. He was still lost in a cloudy fog of confusion.

He adjusted his cap and took a deep breath. *This is it. Ready or not.*

"Ready, sweetie?" his mom called as she knocked on the bathroom door.

"Ready, Mom."

He opened the door, and her eyes filled with tears. She reached out and gave him a hug. "I'm so proud of you, Chase."

But he wasn't feeling proud. He had wanted and expected so much more by now.

He straightened his cap and followed his mom to the car. Apprehensively, he headed to his high school graduation. He had no idea what awaited him. Like a chip from a porcelain plate, he had become disconnected from his once secure future and painfully separate from his childhood friends.

Eager students packed the school auditorium, dressed up nicely underneath their shiny black caps and gowns. Their proud parents sat in the audience and waited for the moment their children would celebrate their first major accomplishment of adulthood. The mood was upbeat and energetic, and Chase tried unsuccessfully to lift his spirits as well. He couldn't help but feel left out. Everyone was ready for their new journeys.

Everyone except him.

As his classmates gathered to receive their diplomas, they chattered excitedly, with many giving each other high fives and big hugs. He spotted Ashley as she ran to Joe and threw her arms around him. Kaitlyn and Kyle held hands while they smiled and chatted with other friends. They all glanced at him once or twice, their faces drawn with concern. No one approached him.

Chase felt the hollow hole inside him expand tenfold. His life was so profoundly empty now. He'd always tried hard to please everyone and make people happy. The end result was that he'd forgotten about himself. And when he tried to shape his own future, he was forced to let everything and everyone in his old life go. Now he waited for what was next.

Soon the graduating class assembled in their seats and listened to the opening remarks and Mary Beth's encouraging but monotonous valedictorian speech. Chase yawned several times out of boredom, but near the end, Mary Beth seemed to perk up, and the last words she uttered brought him back to life.

"We're here for a reason, people. Every person—from your friends, to your teachers, to your parents—has shaped you into who you are today. Without them, you would be an empty shell. So cherish the relationships you've built and strive for connection and collaboration in all you do. And most of all, seize the future and the incredible things awaiting you. Anything is possible. Congratulations, Class!"

Chase glanced at Kaitlyn and saw she was looking at him, too. He smiled. She returned his smile and then looked away. She had always been an important part of his life, and he would never forget everything they'd shared. Now it was time to seize his future and see what was next.

The class lined up to receive their diplomas as

"Pomp and Circumstance" rang through the auditorium. When the last person, Susie Zuccaro, happily clutched her diploma and walked off stage, Chase's graduating class gathered into a large group, much like a swarm of buzzing bees, and threw their caps into the air in a moment of triumph. It wasn't only the end, but also the beginning—in more ways than one.

Soon Chase would pay Willow another visit so he could finally put Darla to rest and put the past behind him.

☯☯☯

Chase was sitting on the couch in his living room when the phone unexpectedly rang. Kaitlyn was crying hysterically and could hardly speak. A part of him wanted to hang up the phone when he heard her voice. After all, she'd made it clear she wanted nothing to do with him, and he didn't appreciate her toying with his heart. But he knew Kaitlyn well. And he knew she wouldn't call him unless she was truly sorry and needed his help. Besides, he had hurt her, too. They were both at fault.

"What's wrong, Kate?"

"I'm so, so sorry for the way I treated you. I can't believe I threw away our friendship. Will you please forgive me?"

"I'm sorry, too. I've really missed you."

"I've missed you, too. I still really need you in my life. Now more than ever."

"Why? Did Kyle break up with you? On graduation

day? The son-of-a—he's such a jerk. He has some nerve! You deserve better."

"Chase, stop! This isn't about Kyle. We didn't break up. In fact, we're going to the movies tonight."

"Well, then, why are you calling *me* with your problems? Shouldn't you be calling your boyfriend for help?"

"No," she said sniffing. "You're the only one who can help me with this."

"I must be pretty special."

"You always were. No one gets me like you do. You've been there for me from the start, and I feel I can trust you with anything."

"You can. Now are you going to tell me what you need help with, or what?"

Kaitlyn didn't answer. The TV blared in the background, and she gasped. "Oh my gosh! They're talking about it again on another channel. Chase, quick, turn on your TV. Channel four."

He grabbed the remote and did as she asked. He saw a photo of a man and then a shot of a teenage girl. He imagined the girl's bloody and bruised face, and the image haunted him. But what bothered him even more was the eerie feeling he got when he heard Kaitlyn gasp. Suddenly an image of two kids—a boy and a girl—appeared in his head. They wore nineteenth century clothing, and the boy defended the little girl from a bully. He got the feeling they were siblings.

On the television, the newscaster's voice announced:

One woman is dead, and a teenage girl is injured

after a severe case of domestic violence. The man responsible? The woman's husband and the girl's father.

Joey Carino was arrested at his home today in Flint on manslaughter and assault charges. Neighbors say they heard shouting coming from the home, followed by several gunshots. They immediately called the police. When the officers arrived, they found Maria Carino dead on the floor with multiple gunshot wounds. Her daughter Sabrina was unconscious and barely breathing. Lacerations covered her body, and she had several broken bones. Relatives of the family say Mr. Carino had a history of alcohol abuse and had been known to assault his wife and daughter on several other occasions, dating back more than fifteen years.

Eighteen-year-old Sabrina is in critical but stable condition at a local hospital. Today, friends and family will gather at the high school for a candlelight vigil to remember Mrs. Carino, a PTO member and dedicated parent, and to pray for the recovery of their classmate, Sabrina.

"How terrible. Do you know this girl?"

"It's her." Kaitlyn sobbed. "It's Sabrina. The one who beat me up in second grade."

"Oh my gosh, Kaitlyn!"

She sniffed again. "All these years I thought she was a mean, nasty bully. It turns out she was a victim, too. Her father had been beating her and her mother for years. It's so sad."

"Yes, it is. Very tragic."

"Don't you see?" Kaitlyn said. "Underneath her

tough exterior, Sabrina was really a scared, lonely girl. She tormented me because she wanted to be in control. She didn't want anyone else to hurt her, so she made sure everyone was afraid of her. They say the abused often become abusers themselves. In one way, she was protecting herself. But in another, she was getting back at her father for what he'd done. She attacked others because she was angry and needed someone to feel the hurt she felt. She took it out on the wrong people."

"Wow, Kaitlyn. You're pretty insightful."

"When I saw the news report, it all made sense to me. So many times we hide our true selves from others. We don't want them to see our weaknesses because we're afraid of being judged and not accepted. I'm guilty, too. But deep down, all we really want is to be liked and to belong somewhere."

"True. I'm still trying to figure out where I belong. So what are you getting at?"

"There's something I have to do, Chase, and I want you to help me."

"Okay. What is it?"

"I want to visit Sabrina in the hospital. I need to make peace with her."

"Seriously? You wanna be nice to your bully?"

"Sabrina's not just a bully. She's a person with feelings. She's got to be hurting right now. Her dad almost killed her, and her mother's dead. I have a sneaking suspicion she doesn't have many friends to lean on. She needs somebody. And I think it should be me."

"You don't have to do this, Kate."

"Yes, I do."

"Are you sure?"

"I am," she said, sniffing. "Will you help me?"

"I know how hard this is for you. I'll do whatever you need."

"I want you to go to the hospital with me tomorrow morning."

"You sure you wanna go so soon? Don't you wanna think about this for a few days?"

"The sooner I do this, the sooner I can put my past behind me."

Chase knew all too well how the past had a way of creeping into the present and wreaking havoc. He longed to put the past behind him soon, too. Maybe helping Kate would lead him to his own path.

"Okay. I know the feeling. How 'bout I pick you up at nine tomorrow?"

"Thanks so much."

He hung up the phone and sat deep in thought for a moment. Kaitlyn's call and the news report had triggered a vision: two children from long ago. Another clue had been laid before him. It was time to decipher its message and uncover the hidden link to his past.

CHAPTER 18
FINDING PEACE

Chase waited at the door of Sabrina's hospital room as Kaitlyn slowly entered. The familiar scent of disinfectant stung his nose, and he could hear the sound of monitors beeping and nurses busily shuffling about in the halls.

Sabrina's eyes were closed, her right one swollen, and black and blue. Chase studied her features: jet-black hair pulled back in a messy ponytail, forehead wrinkled, expression strained. If he hadn't known she was eighteen, he would have guessed she was much older. All the years of torment had apparently aged her.

Kaitlyn approached her bedside and gently took her hand.

He tried to be sympathetic, but all he could think about was what Sabrina had done to Kaitlyn—and a part of him hated her for it. She had no right to treat sweet, kind Kate so cruelly. Sabrina obviously had no respect or empathy for others. No wonder she wasn't very well liked and didn't have many friends. Then again, a monster had raised her. How dare he lay a hand on his wife and child!

This poor girl had been through so much; it was a miracle she was alive at all. She had suffered for years in silence and had now lost her mom at her father's hand. What kind of life would she have now that her mother was dead and her father would go to jail? Lying there in her hospital bed, she looked so frail and weak, not at all like the bully she once was. He didn't know whether to be angry with her or feel sorry for her.

"Hi, Brin," Kaitlyn said softly. She still held Sabrina's hand in hers. "It's Katie. From school all those years ago."

Sabrina stirred in her bed, but didn't open her eyes. Kaitlyn shyly held a vase of colorful wildflowers she had gotten downstairs at the hospital gift shop in her free hand. The bright yellows, oranges, and purples were the only noticeable colors in the dark, cold room.

Kaitlyn let go of Sabrina's hand and set the flowers down on the bedside table. She then walked over to the window and opened the blinds a bit. A beam of sunlight peered in. It seemed the overcast day was indeed clearing.

"I saw the story on the news," she continued. "No one should have to suffer so much. I'm so sorry for all you've been through, Brin."

Sabrina's eyes sprung open. Her facial features hardened. "What the hell are you doing here?" she asked gruffly.

"I thought you could use a friend." Kaitlyn wiped

away a fresh tear.

"Is there something wrong with you?"

"No. Why?"

"I don't understand," Sabrina said loudly as she tossed about in her bed. She moaned in pain, but it didn't seem to stop her from maintaining a tough image. "I was *never* nice to you. I tortured you. Why would you care to see me?"

"Because I know you didn't mean it."

Sabrina laughed. "Oh, yes, I did. I meant every word of it. You're still a piece of trash. A weak little cry baby who can't stand up for herself. Why else would you bring *him*?"

"Stop!" Chase yelled, still standing in the doorway. "You have no right to treat Kaitlyn so badly."

Sabrina stared at him for a minute. "And who the hell are you anyway…her bodyguard?"

"I'm her boyfriend…I mean her best friend."

"Well which is it, Einstein? Are you hooking up with Katie, or are you two friends?"

"I've got this, Chase." Kaitlyn motioned him away.

"Oooh. She spoke," Sabrina taunted.

"Chase and I have been best friends since we were kids. We did the boyfriend-girlfriend thing for a while but decided we were better off as friends. He came here to support me."

"Well isn't he nice?" Sabrina folded her arms.

"You should really try it sometime," Kaitlyn advised. "You know, being nice to people."

"Oh, really?" Sabrina said, smoothing her hair back with her hand. "Well, guess what? I did. And where did it get me? Here. I tried for years to be nice to my father so he wouldn't beat me and my mom. All I ever got in return was a black eye. I told him I loved him once. You know what he said? He said, *'I could never love a worthless piece of trash like you.'* Then he punched me real hard in the stomach."

"I'm sorry," Kaitlyn said.

"And now my mom is dead! She tried to stand up to him and he bloody *killed* her! Who does that crap? Who the heck tortures their own family?"

Sabrina's voice cracked, and she turned her head to her bedside table to grab a cup of water. She gulped. Slowly, she ran her finger along a yellow daisy.

"You brought me…flowers?" she asked, her voice shaking.

"Yes, I did."

"Why?"

"Because I wanted you to know someone cared and you're not alone."

"But I beat you up… and called you names…and scared the living daylights out of you. And instead of hating me, you brought me flowers. It doesn't make any sense."

"Sabrina, what you did to me was awful. I was terrified of you, and you made me feel like a horrible person. But when I saw the news report, I understood. You weren't only a mean, heartless bully. You were a victim too. You did those things to me because you didn't know any other way to relate to people."

Kaitlyn drew in a sharp breath and continued. "You wanted to feel in control of some part of your life because your home life was so painful. He made you feel weak and afraid and insecure. Putting on a tough front was your way of coping. It made you feel powerful, strong—unlike how you felt at home. Was it right to treat me the way you did? Absolutely not. You can't fix violence with more violence. You can't end pain with more pain. And, as my mother always told me, two wrongs never make a right."

A tear gently trickled down her cheek. "But I'm here to say I *forgive* you. I want to make peace with the past. I want you to know you can have a better future. Everyone deserves a second chance."

Sabrina stared at Kate in disbelief. Chase couldn't tell if she was about to yell, cry, or do both. He joined Kaitlyn at Sabrina's bedside and put his arm around her. "C'mon, Kate. You've done all you can here. It's time to go."

She nodded, and they slowly turned and began to walk away.

"Wait," Sabrina called out.

Chase and Kaitlyn both turned to face Sabrina once again. Tears were streaming down her face. "Thank you," she croaked. "I don't know what else to say...but…thank you."

"You're welcome," Kaitlyn said. She walked over to Sabrina and reached out to give her a big hug.

The two embraced like old friends and sobbed together.

"You are a beautiful person, Kaitlyn," Sabrina said. "A true angel."

"I hope you find some peace in your life, Brin. No

one deserves what you went through."

"Thank you." Sabrina wiped her eyes. "And for the record, you're right. I never meant all those nasty things I said and did to you. If you want the truth, I actually *admired* you. I wanted to be like you, to have a secure happy life and a stable family that loved me. I was secretly jealous."

"Really?"

"Yes, really. But do you know what I wanted most of all?"

"No, I don't."

"I wanted to be your friend, Katie."

"Well, you sure had a funny way of showing it."

They all laughed. "I didn't think you would ever want to be friends with someone like me," Sabrina said.

"Try me. I can be a really good friend, and I'm a great listener. Ask Chase."

"She's the best," he agreed. He patted Kaitlyn on the shoulder. "She's like a sister to me. You should give her a chance."

"Deal," Sabrina said, extending her hand.

Kaitlyn grabbed it and then leaned in for another hug.

"Take care of yourself."

"It looks like I'm gonna have to. My dad's going to jail for life, and my mom's dead. I'm all alone. It's just me now."

"No, it's not," Kaitlyn corrected. "You have me."

Sabrina wiped away more tears. "Thank you," she whispered.

Chase and Kaitlyn walked out of the hospital room

with their arms around each other. The air around Chase felt lighter, and so did he. He could only imagine what a relief this visit had been for Kaitlyn. She'd not only faced her past and her fears, but she'd also brought comfort to Sabrina. He had witnessed a new and unlikely friendship form right before his eyes. It was interesting how connected people were without even realizing it.

An older woman with graying hair rushed by and bumped into Kate. "Excuse me," she cried, stopping in her tracks. She stared at Kaitlyn.

"Oh, hello," Kaitlyn said.

"My dear. I'm so glad you and your brother are speaking again. I knew he would take care of you. He always has."

"Thank you," Kate replied.

"Come see me again sometime," the lady said, smiling. "Your brother could use some help, too. His past is about to reveal itself." She looked at Chase and grinned. "Have you talked to her lately? You know, the girl from the park. You need to find her." Then she was on her way.

Chase shivered. Had Kaitlyn told her about the girl? "What was that all about?" he asked.

"Oh, she's the psychic I told you about. Seems she's happy we've made amends, bro."

Chase laughed. "I'm happy, too. Kate, you're amazing. I'm so lucky to have you in my life."

"I'm the lucky one. You've stood by me through everything—even while dealing with your own inner demons. Thanks for supporting me, Chase."

"Of course. Best friends look out for each other."

He kissed her softly on the forehead. “Let me take you home now. There’s still something I need to do. You confronted your demons. Now it’s time to confront mine.”

CHAPTER 19
LIFE AFTER LIFE

Chase didn't walk the familiar path in Lincoln Park this time. Instead, he ran. He wanted to get to his special place near the pond and find the girl. A sense of urgency drew him to her as if his future depended on it. The psychic knew something about her. He had to find out what it was.

His heart pounded like a man on a hunt, but he panted like the one being hunted. He reached the pond breathless, and his heart thumped loudly when he saw her standing there as if she were waiting for him. She wore a simple green cotton dress and jean jacket, and was far more beautiful than he'd noticed before. He couldn't put his finger on the reason why; all he knew was that her shiny brown hair and welcoming brown eyes beckoned him.

"You're in a hurry to see me," she said, smiling brightly.

"How do you know I'm here to see you?"

"Because I know you. I knew you'd come back for me. I came here to see you, too."

"Really?"

"Really. I'm so glad you remember me. Now we can get on with things. We can have the relationship we deserve to have."

"There's one problem. I still don't know who you are. I can't get involved with you without knowing the facts."

A look of surprise spread across her face. "You really don't know me?"

"Nope."

"Okay. Well, what do you want to know then?"

She sat down on Chase's favorite park bench and motioned for him to join her. He took a seat beside her as the butterflies in his stomach began to spread their wings. His stomach growled, and she giggled.

"Do I make you nervous?" she asked.

"You make me something…I'm not sure what."

"I'll take that as a compliment."

She smiled and took his hand in hers. Her warmth sent tiny tingles along his spine that left him speechless.

"Don't be shy," she said. "What are your questions?"

He squeezed her hand and looked down at the ground. "Well, for starters, am I really a part of your past? And how do you know for sure? I could be someone else who reminds you of this person."

"You are really a part of my past. You're a part of me. I know this because you are undeniably, unmistakably you. I could recognize you anywhere."

"Then why did you run away that night when you were watching me in the dark? And why did you keep making me chase you?"

"Simple. I was afraid. I didn't know if you would remember me. Plus, I watched you with a pretty blonde girl on several occasions. I saw you hug her. You two looked very close. I didn't want to interfere."

"Oh. You must mean Kaitlyn. She's my friend."

"She looked like a lot more than a friend to me."

Chase detected a bit of jealousy in her voice.

"We've been best friends since childhood. She was my girlfriend once, but that's over now."

"Good." She nodded with approval. "I didn't want to come to you unless I thought you were ready."

"Ready for what?"

"Ready for me. Ready for us."

"But there is no *us*. Just because we were young childhood friends or something doesn't mean we're in love or anything."

"Aren't we?" She raised an eyebrow.

Chase thought hard. He'd felt something for her the other night and still did now. But he could be getting caught up in some fantasy. He seemed to have a knack for doing so. Besides, no matter how hard he tried, he still couldn't remember her. She had claimed to be his wife, but he knew she couldn't be. It was impossible.

Unless…

Could there be something to this whole past lives thing?

"How can I love you when I don't even know your

name?" he asked.

"Love doesn't require labels or names. It's a feeling."

She rested her head on his shoulder and stroked his face. Chase thought he should discourage such behavior. She was still a stranger to him, after all. But oddly, he welcomed her touch. Or rather, he craved it.

"Okay. Then tell me more about how we know each other."

"You tell me."

"I would. But as I've said, I don't remember you. Are you sure we really know each other? You're not messing with me, are you?"

"Positive," she insisted. "So tell me, why did you break up with Kaitlyn?"

"Kaitlyn's amazing."

"But?"

"Well…you see…I couldn't shake the feeling I was supposed to be with someone else. Someone more like—"

"Me?" she interrupted, looking up at him.

"What? No…I mean…I don't know. I don't know you well enough to know if you're my type."

Chase looked into her eyes and couldn't help but become lost in them. She had somehow cast a spell on him, and he magically fell into a trance. He would soon be totally in her control.

A gentle breeze blew as he became caught up in the moment. The air smelled fresher, the sunlight was brighter, and he was more alive than he'd been in a very long time. The passion built within him, and he looked longingly at her plump lips. The desire to press his body against hers and kiss her was overwhelming.

"Then why are you looking at me like you want to kiss me?" she asked.

Her words rocked him to the core. She was absolutely right. He had only really known her for a short time, at least as far as he remembered, but he already felt a powerful connection to her. He wanted to kiss her so badly, and he fought like heck not to.

"So are you going to tell me?" he asked, changing the subject.

"Tell you what?"

"Where I know you from and what your name is."

"Not yet."

"Seriously? What kind of game are you playing here?"

"No game. In time, you'll remember everything."

"What if I don't? What if I never remember who you are? Or even worse, what if I'm not the person you think I am? Then what? You're plain frustrating! I have no desire to be involved with someone who won't even be honest with me."

Chase was angry at her evasiveness, but he couldn't deny the passion he felt for her any longer. An unseen force took over him as he grabbed her shoulders and pulled her toward him, his heart racing. She closed her eyes and leaned in. Their lips met fiercely, and they held each other tight. Chase's soul erupted into an explosion of fireworks.

"If you don't want to be involved with me, then why did you kiss me?" she asked.

"I don't know. You're confusing me."

"I think it's pretty clear," she said confidently. "You want me."

She was right. He did.

He pressed his lips against hers again, and the heat rose between them. Her kisses were sweet yet also mature and sexy, and he couldn't deny he was already falling for her. He felt exhilarated, rejuvenated. Like someone had woken him up from a long, deep slumber. He never wanted the moment to end. It was like in his dreams, only this girl was real. She was right here with him, kissing him like no woman on Earth had ever kissed him before. She ran her fingers through his hair and planted soft kisses on his neck.

"Amazing," she said.

"Yes, it was."

"Do you remember now?"

She stood quietly staring into his eyes, the desire burning within her. He recognized her hunger, but she was still a mystery to him. He really had no idea how or where they could have met.

"I'm sorry. I'm afraid I don't."

A look of disappointment came over her face, and her bottom lip pouted slightly. "I have to go," she said sadly.

"No. Please don't go," he begged. "Everyone keeps leaving me, and it really hurts."

"What hurts is knowing you have no memory of who I am. I can't believe you could forget me so easily."

"Maybe if you kiss me again, I'll remember."

"No. Next time we kiss, I want it to be for real. I want to be certain you really know me and you're not just imagining someone else or living out some fantasy."

She was right. She deserved better than what he could give her right now. Much like him, Kaitlyn, and the rest of the world, she wanted it all. And if she couldn't have it, she was prepared to walk away.

"Can we meet again?" Chase asked.

"Perhaps."

"Maybe tomorrow?"

"We'll see."

"Okay. I have a couple of things I need to do today. But I will come back here tomorrow, and we can try again."

She nodded, then turned for the path. When she disappeared out of sight, Chase pulled out his cell and dialed Dr. Whitgard.

"Whitgard here."

"Hey, Doc. It's Chase. I need a favor."

"What is it, dear boy?"

"Do you have time for a quick hypnosis session? There's someone I want to remember."

"Okay. You're in luck. I finished lunch and was about to run some errands. Head to my office. I'll meet you there in fifteen minutes."

"Thanks, Doc."

"You're very welcome. I'm so excited to see what we can reveal today."

"Me, too."

☯☯☯

Dr. Whitgard sat at his desk, waiting for Chase

when he arrived. The doc's eyes were aglow with wonder, and his usually ratty hair was pulled back into a long ponytail.

"C'mon. C'mon," he said, motioning animatedly. "Follow me back."

Chase followed him to his office and got comfortable on his couch. He was ready to find out more about the mystery girl and his connection to her. They got started right away on the relaxation exercises, and Dr. Whitgard urged him to think of the girl. Chase pictured her compassionate brown eyes and sweet smile. They were standing in the park facing each other like earlier today. He felt happy and in love. He leaned in to kiss her, but suddenly she burst into flames. He jumped back.

"Chase? What happened?" Dr. Whitgard asked with concern. "Did you remember anything? Did you get her name?"

"No. The girl was there, but when I went to kiss her, she burst into flames and disappeared."

"I see. Highly unusual. Let me think. How should we proceed?"

"I don't know. You tell me."

He put his hand on his forehead for a few minutes, grunting and grumbling as if he were in search of something. "Aha," he said, raising a finger. "I have an idea. I want you to concentrate on the flames. Stare at them and see what comes to you."

Chase did as he asked, and the flames morphed into the reoccurring scene from the plane crash. He was in his seat as the plane once again plummeted toward the earth below. It was a scene he knew so well but longed to permanently erase from his mind. This had gone on too long! He helplessly clutched the seat arms as the aircraft smashed into the ground in a fiery explosion. He felt the heat of the fire as it engulfed the plane and surrounded his body. His skin burned, and he let out a scream.

"Talk to me, Chase. Tell me what you see."

Chase described the scene and the sensation to Dr. Whitgard.

"How very odd," the doc said. "Your mind is behaving as if you were actually in a plane crash. Are you sure you were never in a fire or crash of any kind? An automobile accident, perhaps?"

"No, I wasn't. I even asked my mom and she denied it."

"But did you ask yourself?"

"Why would I ask myself? I was a kid, and my mom wouldn't lie to me. If she says nothing ever happened, then it didn't."

"Maybe your mother doesn't know it happened."

"What? What you're suggesting doesn't make any sense. Why wouldn't my mother not know what happened to her own child?"

"Sometimes the soul knows things the mind does not."

"I'm sorry. I don't follow you." Chase's head now spun, and he thought he might faint.

"Your life is about more than your current existence. There are so many facets to Chase. Each is intertwined within you, some buried deeply. They are all a part of you."

"Doc, are you trying to say what I think you are?"

"Have you ever heard of past lives, my boy?"

"In movies and books, but they're not real, are they?"

He really wasn't sure what was real anymore. His life and recent events had led him to question reality and everything he once believed to be true.

"And how do you know what's real? How do you know you haven't lived before?"

Chase thought for a moment and allowed his logic to trickle in. "I would remember, wouldn't I?"

"Maybe. Or maybe not. Instead, you could see visions of a crash you were in or of a life you once had."

Chase's heart soared as he realized what this could mean. It all seemed so unbelievable, but made sense at the same time. "Is there any way to remember these past lives?"

"Yes, we can do a past lives regression. I tried it once with you, but you saw only black. Why don't we try again and see what happens? You're more receptive to it now, so we may get something."

"I'm ready," Chase said.

A warm, eager rush of blood spread to his face. If he had lived before, he had to know more. Determined to find the missing pieces of his psyche, he closed his eyes, and Dr. Whitgard guided him to his destination.

Blackness penetrated his eyelids once again, but this time, he stayed patient and hopeful. He breathed slowly and deeply as he waited for something more. After a few minutes, the darkness began to fade. A vibrant blue glow replaced it, followed by thousands of twinkling stars. They welcomed him to another world, another time.

First, he saw a clear image of a nine-year-old boy. The child sweat profusely as he worked diligently in a cotton mill, cleaning fluff from a large machine. His clothing suggested the boy had lived sometime in the nineteenth century, possibly in England. Heavy tan trousers exposed his calves, and he sported knee-high socks, a white cotton shirt, and a brown beanie. Beside him, a little girl tied the ends of the cotton. She looked at him with sad eyes, which he recognized immediately as Kaitlyn's eyes. *Was she his sister after all?*

Next, he saw Darla. She wore a beautiful wedding gown like the one in his vision, and the two of them stood happily in a garden overlooking a waterfall. He had seen this all before. It had felt so real. *Was it?*

The scene morphed into a vision of a rainy day in the park. As he splashed through muddy puddles, he spotted a beautiful woman in the distance. He squinted to see her better, but the pouring rain obstructed his view. *Was she Darla? Had he shared a life with Darla in another time and place?*

Urgency bubbled within him, and he could no longer contain the rush of adrenaline and emotions. "Dr. Whitgard," he interrupted. "I'm sorry to cut this short, but there's something I have to do."

He had to see Darla's granddaughter Willow as soon as possible. She was the only one who could confirm what he suspected.

"Excellent! You remembered something?"

"Yes, I think I did. I might finally know who I

really am." Chase sprang from his seat and extended his hand. "Thank you, Doc. It's time to reclaim my past."

☯☯☯

Chase got into his car after his session with Dr. Whitgard. He was more determined than ever to uncover the truth. He pulled up Willow's address on his cell phone, and then sped to her house, ready to finally meet her. He hoped she was home this time.

Trees whizzed by. Cars became a blur. The world around him became quiet and still. Chase's mind drifted, much like when he was in hypnosis. He found himself unexpectedly sucked into a world where Darla was alive, and Willow would lead him to her. He imagined what Willow would say to him.

"My grandmother didn't die. She was often confused with her twin sister Marla. She's the one who died in the plane crash. My grandmother is right upstairs. Do you want to meet her?"

He envisioned Darla gracefully climbing down the stairs, her wavy brown hair brushing against her shoulders. She would look like she did in her twenties, wearing the gorgeous red lace dress he'd last seen her in during his prom dream. She would smile at him, take his hand and kiss him. He would never again let her go.

A horn behind him honked loudly. He was apparently sitting at a stoplight that had turned green. As he started to accelerate, the man behind him shouted curse words out his window and blew by him.

What is wrong with me?

Willow had never even met him, and now he was about to barge into her house and insist she tell him about her grandmother—a woman he believed he'd shared another life with. Was he going crazy? Had school, his nightmares, and his girl trouble finally made him crack?

The more he thought rationally about it, the more he realized Willow would be unlikely to share much with him. If someone arrived at his door asking questions about his relatives, he would refuse to answer and send them on their way. It was the most likely scenario. Yet he still felt compelled to travel on. He was actually going to do this. Wild as it was, he was going to knock on Willow's door again and try to get some answers.

Rain smashed against his windshield, which triggered the scene that had begun to unfold in Dr. Whitgard's office. Images from a long-forgotten place materialized before his eyes.

Chase walked his dog, a loyal golden retriever, through the trails at the park. The rain began to fall, and before long, it came down in buckets. Lightning illuminated the sky, and a loud crash of thunder rumbled above. He picked up his pace, determined to get to the car as quickly as possible.

He stopped abruptly when he saw her. She danced in the rain as if she had never seen or felt it before. A huge smile spread across her face, and she giggled joyfully. He stood there, silently watching her. The soaking wet girl possessed a beauty and charisma he had never before witnessed. She mesmerized him.

Their eyes met, and he stumbled, his dog's leash falling from his hand. The dog ran eagerly to her, and she pet him lovingly. Chase wanted her to touch him, too. He joined his pooch at her side, and they gazed into each other's eyes for several minutes. The hair on the back of his neck stood on end. The electricity between them was immeasurable. She held out her hand and he took it in his.

"I'm Darla."

"Hello, Darla. Do you want to dry off and get some dinner with me?"

"Sure." She grinned. "But first you need to tell me your name."

They laughed loudly, and Chase's face turned red.

"Don't be embarrassed," she said. "Maybe this will help."

She planted a soft kiss on his cheek, which left him wanting so much more. No woman had ever had this effect on him. She was the one he'd been waiting for.

Chase pulled into the apartment complex where Darla's granddaughter lived and drove past several buildings, all brown brick with forest green shutters. The grounds were neatly landscaped and maintained, with blue spruce trees and hostas framing each building. A small park in the center contained a playground set, picnic tables, and a tiny manmade pond. The peaceful, tranquil setting reminded him of a campground he'd once visited as a child with his father. Past the park, he spotted building number seven and quickly parked the car in a nearby lot. He sprang out of the driver's seat, ready to face what was next.

An overcast sky darkened the parking lot, and a few tiny raindrops brushed against his face. Urgency overcame him, and he ran to Willow's unit with a marathon athlete's vigor. He reached unit 727, breathless and panting. His heart raced from fear, excitement, and anticipation. He hoped Willow wouldn't slam the door in his face.

He combed his hand through his hair and eagerly rang the doorbell. Not long after, he saw some movement through the window, and someone cautiously peeked through a tiny peephole at the top of the green steel door. Much to his surprise, a beautiful young girl with brown hair soon answered. His heart stopped when he saw her face: *the mystery girl from the park.*

"It's you," he cried.

"It's you," she repeated. She threw her arms around him. "I knew you'd come for me, Rob."

Chase's heart sank. The girl from the park was indeed Willow, but she still believed he was someone else. He felt silly for getting so caught up in some fantasy and for kissing her like she meant something to him. He'd gotten carried away and let his dreams of Darla cloud his judgment. He owed this poor girl an apology for leading her on. He tried to speak, but the only sound he managed was a faint squeak.

"Are you okay, Rob?" she asked, her eyes wide. "Maybe you'd better come in for a drink of water."

He stepped into her foyer, and she hurried off into the kitchen to get him a drink. So many thoughts rushed through his mind. Should he pretend to be this Rob character? He did find Willow incredibly attractive, and she looked so much like her grandmother, Darla. Plus, she seemed really into him. Maybe they could actually have a relationship.

No, he couldn't deceive her. She would be furious when she found out the truth. He couldn't start a relationship based on a lie. He had to tell her he wasn't Rob.

"Why did you call me Rob?"

She smiled and handed him a drink. "Because it's your name. I could call you Robbie, if you'd prefer."

"I'm sorry. I'm not Rob or Robbie. My name's Chase."

"Aww. So cute." She softly rubbed his shoulder with her hand. "I like the name, Chase. I'm Willow, by the way."

She reached out and shook his hand with the delicateness of a flower. Chase's knees became weak, and electricity coursed through his body. He felt like he was going to pass out. She motioned toward the sofa.

"Please sit down, Robbie. You look pale, like you've seen a ghost or something."

Chase sort of felt like he had. The resemblance was uncanny. He had noticed the resemblance in the park, but now it was even more prominent. He found himself daydreaming about Darla and the dance they'd shared in his dreams.

"I need to talk to you about Darla, your grandmother. I think I may have a connection to her."

A big smile spread across her face. "Of course. What do you want to know?"

"How did she and your grandfather meet?"

She clapped her hands. "This is such a great love story! Like the kind you would see in the movies. Do you want some popcorn? A Pepsi maybe?"

"What? Um…no thanks. I'm not hungry."

"Very well then. It was a rainy day in the park. My grandmother had gone there to celebrate after receiving a full-tuition scholarship for college. She was excited to become a teacher. The skies turned dark quickly, but instead of returning to her car, she decided to embrace the moment and have a little fun. She let the rain soak her while she spun and danced. Meanwhile, my grandfather walked his dog through the trails and he noticed her. She danced in the rain like she was feeling it for the first time. He thought she was so beautiful and intriguing. Their eyes met, and it was love at first sight."

Chase nodded his head. "Yes, I remember the same thing…I know this is going to sound really crazy, Willow. But I believe I'm your grandfather."

She laughed heartily and plopped herself down on the couch next to him. "Do you?"

"You probably think I'm nuts, huh?"

"Not nuts. But you're actually wrong."

She scooted closer until their bodies were up against each other. Then she kissed his ear with tiny, loving nibbles. Tingles traveled down his spine. He desperately wanted to kiss her again, but to do so would be wrong. He didn't know this girl yet, and even more importantly, she could be his granddaughter.

"Does that feel good, Robbie?" she whispered, breathlessly. She ran her fingers through his hair and began kissing his neck.

"I can't do this."

She stopped kissing him and looked up with sad, longing eyes. "Why not?"

She sat in Chase's lap and wrapped her arms around him. He could smell her perfume, a combination of fresh cut roses and lilies. He wanted to rest his head on her shoulder and breathe in her scent. He longed to run his fingers along her neck and kiss her. But giving in to his urges would be so wrong.

"Willow, don't you realize what's happening here? I could be your dead grandfather reincarnated. I know you were born after he died, but we can't have a relationship, no matter how we feel about each other."

A tear formed in the corner of her eye. "But I'm in love with you."

"You can't be in love with your own grandfather."

She wrinkled her forehead and thought for a moment. Her brown eyes glazed over as if she were staring off into space.

"Willow? Are you all right?"

"I understand your concerns. But you're not my grandfather in *this* life. And you weren't back then either."

"What do you mean?"

She cleared her throat and looked at him. "Robert Chambers died in a plane crash with his wife in 1973. It was a fiery crash, and the plane exploded on impact. There were no survivors. All of the passengers and the crew were killed."

"Yes. You're right. Your mom, Kendra, must have

told you the story."

She shook her head in disagreement. "My mom was Kendra. Her mother, Darla, was my grandmother."

"Yes." Chase was relieved she hadn't totally lost it. Maybe she was finally understanding why they couldn't be together.

"Darla was married to Robert Chambers, my grandfather."

"Correct," he said, feeling more relieved. Willow had come back to reality.

She stood and paced the floors. "But that's not how I know about the plane crash." She walked back and forth in front of the couch. "My mother didn't tell me what happened."

"Then how do you know?"

Willow stopped pacing and stood in front of him. A tear slowly trickled down her face, and she quickly wiped it with the back of her hand. She swallowed hard. "I know," she said softly, gazing deep into his eyes, "because I was there."

"What?"

"I was there. You were, too. I'm Darla, and you're my husband Robert."

Chase's head pounded, and his thoughts became jumbled. How could Willow be her own grandmother? He tried to keep an open mind, but had carried this all too far. He had let his fantasies of Darla cloud his judgment and muffle his thinking. He had to clear his head so he could make sense of everything. He rose from the couch and headed for the door. Willow followed him. She grabbed his arm, and a thrill ran through him. He wanted to kiss her.

"Don't leave, Robert."

He turned to face her and nearly gave in to the undeniable passion stirring inside him. But his rational mind put a stop to it. He had to stay focused. His days of chasing impossible dreams stopped here. "What you're suggesting doesn't make any sense. It's so unbelievable. I feel like my head could explode at any moment. Besides, I have a life here…today."

"With Kaitlyn?"

"With whichever girl I decide is right for me."

"What if *I'm* right for you?"

Chase stared at her. She was perfect for him—everything he had always hoped for. He found it hard to ignore the incredible chemistry they shared. All he had to do was stand near her, and an exhilarating wave nearly brought him to his knees. She was a magnet, drawing him to her.

He fought hard against the pull. His mind told him to walk away, to put the past in the past and focus on a plausible future. But his soul wanted her. It was as if they belonged together. Except for one detail: she believed she was her own grandmother.

"You can't deny your feelings for me," she said. "You may claim we can't get involved, but we already are. I meant what I said to you, Robert."

"What did you say?"

"Love will always find a way."

Chase shivered. *Love will always find a way.*

His intellect and his soul drew their swords in a final battle. A flicker of awareness sliced through him.

He needed to make sense of everything in a way he had never considered before.

Rationality let go, and he allowed his mind to flash back to the dream of Darla in her red lace prom dress. She had said those very words to him. Willow had said the same thing to him in the park. But she couldn't have known Darla had uttered them. It was *his* dream.

Unless.

He looked at Willow with a puzzled expression as he finally connected the dots.

She smiled. "You know it, too. You can feel it."

"Feel what?"

"You're Robert, my husband. And I'm Darla, your wife."

His knees felt weak, and he began to stumble. Willow reached out and held him tight. He took a deep breath and relaxed in her arms. He belonged there. He was sure of it now. What was happening to him? Had his dream become a reality? Could this really be true?

"It's true," she said, as if reading his mind. "We made a pact to come back to this life and find each other again. And here we are."

"How's this possible?"

"I can't answer your question, but I can enlighten you a bit. Our connection is strong. It survives across time, worlds, and even death. We can find each other no matter where we are."

Chase scratched his head and furrowed his brow. "I'm confused."

"Remember when we were dancing at the prom? I wore a red lace dress and you begged me never to leave you. We shared a magical kiss."

"It was only a dream, Willow. Besides, how could you know about my dream? You weren't even there."

"Oh, but I was. I was in your dreams. We were really together."

"I don't understand." Chase's head was beginning to pound again. "How can you visit me in my dreams?"

"It's called astral travel. Your soul leaves your body when you sleep at night and can travel anywhere it wants. Of course, I traveled to you. I couldn't stay away. You're my soulmate."

His head spun with all of the unbelievable stuff she had shared. Was he having another one of his bizarre dreams? He pinched himself and tried hard to wake up. Nothing happened. He was still there with Willow.

"Okay. Let's suppose you did astral travel to me. Then explain how you could possibly be Darla Chambers, your own grandmother? That would mean you were Kendra's mom *and* her daughter."

"Yes, I am one and the same. After I died, I wanted so much to be part of my daughter's life. It pained me to see my little girl growing up without a mom. I tried to be there for her, but it's different when you're not a part of the physical world. I watched over her; I was present during all of her milestones. But she couldn't see me or touch me. So, when she grew up, I decided I would come back to Earth as her daughter."

"Hmm. Strangely, what you suggest does make some sense. But if you knew all of this, then why didn't you come out and tell me who you were in the park the first time? What was the point of keeping my past from me for so long?"

"There are rules, Robert. Or should I call you Chase?"

"What kind of rules? What are you talking about?"

"When you die, you become privy to all sorts of information. You can choose to come back to Earth or stay in the afterlife to help others. When you do come back here, you do so with the understanding you may not remember who you once were. You only remember when it benefits you, when it's best for your soul. For this reason, you're sworn to secrecy about other souls' past lives."

Chase raised an eyebrow. She didn't seem to notice and continued.

"Even if you know who they are, you can't tell them until the right time. If you do, it could affect the course of their lives and have serious repercussions. So I couldn't say anything. I had to let you figure it out for yourself. When I thought you were on the verge of remembering, it was okay for me to help you along."

Past lives? Reincarnation? These were concepts Chase had never believed in. But when Willow explained them, they actually seemed possible. Even Dr. Whitgard had embraced these concepts and worked hard to reveal Chase's past and former life with Darla.

"This is all so much to absorb." He felt lightheaded and thought he might pass out. "I need to lie down."

"Sure," she said, grabbing a pillow from the couch.

Chase plopped himself down on the soft, red plush couch and leaned his weary head into the white shag pillow. "I still don't get how any of this is possible. It's so bizarre and incredible. How can this be?"

"Like I said, I don't know the answer." She stroked his face. "All I know is I love you. And I'm so happy we found each other again."

She looked at him with those mesmerizing eyes, the ones he had seen so many times before in his dreams. His heart became filled with an undeniable love. Scenes and images from a time long ago flashed before him. Suddenly, he remembered every vivid detail of his life with Darla Chambers, a life cut short by a fiery plane crash in 1973.

"I never thought I'd see you again, Darla."

"I always knew we'd be together again, Robert. We made a promise."

They held each other tight. Two souls had found their way back to each other through space and time. Chase was home at last.

"There's one thing, though," she said.

"What?"

"In this lifetime, I think it's best if we call each other Willow and Chase. You know, so it's less confusing for people."

"Of course. It will be our little secret."

Outside the window, a gentle rain began to fall, washing away all that had plagued Chase's mind and soul during this lifetime. Through the clouds, a radiant beam of sunlight shone down, forming the perfect rainbow. The storm was over: no more fiery crashes, no more questions, no more mysterious dreams. Only him and her.

Willow leaned in. Her lips touched his softly, and

they kissed passionately and deeply. The magic between them was exactly as he'd always remembered it. He had found his dream girl once more; only this time, she was no longer a dream. She was a part of him and had been there in his heart all along. Love had found a way.

"I love you, Willow." Chase held her tight, their bodies blending together as one. "You'll always be a part of me."

ABOUT THE AUTHOR

Award-winning author Deanna Kahler is a passionate writer with more than twenty years of professional experience. Her work has appeared in numerous newsletters and magazines and on websites across the country. She began writing as a young child and enjoys the opportunity to reach others and make a difference in their lives.

Deanna holds a bachelor's degree in communication arts from Oakland University in Rochester, Michigan, where she graduated with honors. She lives with her husband and daughter in the Detroit area and enjoys writing, dancing, walking, and visiting parks in her spare time.

For more information about the author, please visit www.deannakahler.com.

Made in the USA
Columbia, SC
20 June 2017